AND SHADOWS WILL FALL

A LOVING HUSBAND STORY

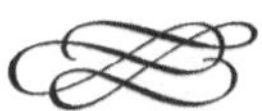

MEREDITH ALLARD

"Keep your face always toward the sunshine—
and shadows will fall behind you."

— WALT WHITMAN

And Shadows Will Fall

Copyright © 2024 Meredith Allard

All rights reserved. No part of this publication may be reproduced, distributed, or transmitted in any form or by any means, including photocopying, recording, or other electronic or mechanical methods, without the written permission of the publisher, except in the case of brief quotations embodied in book reviews and other noncommercial uses permitted by copyright law.

Cover design by Jenny Quinlan

Copperfield Press

ISBN: 979-8-218-41602-7

And Shadows Will Fall/Meredith Allard – 1st paperback edition 2024

{1. Fiction. 2. Salem Witch Trials—Fiction. 3. Contemporary Romance—Fiction. 4. Paranormal Romance Series—Fiction. 5. Contemporary American—Fiction. 6. Paranormal Witches—Fiction. 7. Massachusetts—Fiction.} I. Title

Publisher's Note: This is a work of fiction. Names, characters, businesses, places, and events portrayed in this book are a product of the author's imagination or used in a fictitious way. Any similarity to real persons, living or dead, places, events, or locales is entirely coincidental.

PROLOGUE

Tis August and sweltering heat hovers six feet above ground whilst humidity weighs me down, into my grave, I think. Where else can I be but six feet under without my Lizzie? I wipe perspiration from my cheek with the back of my hand, my handkerchief nowhere to be found. And then I realize. Tis not perspiration I wipe but tears, salty like the sea. I pace outside the dungeon, a futile attempt to release a fury so pent up I feel I will combust. Lizzie is behind that wall, trapped in that God-forsaken place, she and our unborn child.

"Oh, Lizzie," I say aloud. "How has it come to this? We were but a day from leaving this horror behind. How did we get caught up in the madness? I was so certain we would escape."

I shake my fist at the prison wall. "I told you we should leave. But you were intent on staying until after our babe was born." I scream despite the odd glances of passers-by. "I should have grabbed you by the arms and forced you to leave!" I slump to the ground, a heap of untended clothing, banging my head against the wall. "I shall fix it, my love. And then we shall be free."

Humidity steals the air, leaving hollow hotness in my lungs. People stare in my direction. From their contorted features I think they believe I am possessed by Satan. Perhaps I am.

I am light-headed and for a moment I forget where I am. But the bliss of forgetting is gone as quickly as it arrived and I am certain I shall vomit. I press my hands into the prison wall with whatever strength I can muster. There is just this one wall between us, after all, and I pray for the strength of one hundred men so I can knock this barrier down and break her free. Tis but one wall, but tis enough. Tis an ocean I cannot cross without drowning, taking Lizzie down with me. There is no end to this accursement. I know it in my bones.

I am increasingly aware of the sights and sounds of life surrounding me. Horses gallop at the commands of their drivers. Blacksmiths hammer and bakers shout, waving their fresh-scented goods above their heads. Scattered bird songs punctuate the air like distant ripples. Snippets of half-heard conversations float above my head.

I turn away like a child, believing that if I cannot see them then they cannot see me. Yet there is no avoiding them. Three well-dressed men linger, men familiar to me, business acquaintances of Father, I think. In my muddled state I cannot remember their names. Father warned me that we have become a topic of conversation amongst Town and Village. With Lizzie accused of witchcraft and languishing in prison, others look for justification for our misfortunes.

I try to ignore the men but they speak loudly, wishing for me to overhear, I am certain.

"Why, there's young Wentworth," says the first man "He shouldn't be sitting there, of all places, I'm sure."

"Perhaps he's lost his mind. His wife has been named a witch, you know," says the second.

"Mistress Wentworth a witch? Never," says the third. "Anyone will say she's a God-fearing woman. A Quaker, they say, but there's no help for that, I reckon."

"A Quaker, indeed? That's unfortunate. Who says she's a Quaker?" says the second man.

"Tis only what I heard. You never know what is right and what is false in such matters."

Yet tis all worth repeating, I think angrily.

"No matter what anyone says, I shan't believe she is a witch," says the third. "I have signed my name to the petition the Wentworths are sending

round stating that I have never seen her act in any way that put her in league with the Devil."

"You best be careful, Davies," the first man says. "People may think you are in communication with Satan if word gets round that you signed the petition." He leans close to the other two, his voice still loud enough for me to hear. "They say tis her very own brother who accused her, her brother and his wife. Why would a brother accuse his sister of Devilry if there were no truth to it?"

I could name a hundred reasons, I want to yell.

"Maybe Mistress Wentworth is controlling your mind," the first man continues. "They can do that you know, the witches. These vassals of Evil work their malignant magic on unsuspecting innocents until they no longer know which is the righteous way." From the corner of my mind, I see the speaker nod toward me. "Perhaps she controls his mind."

"I agree with Smithers," the third man says. "Those who do the Devil's bidding cloud your judgment, piece by piece, til they have turned your thoughts to mush. Then you sign your name to that unholy book, pledging your soul to Satan. Once you are bound to the Devil even God cannot help you."

The men wander away, still huddled in their conversation. Suddenly, like a woodpecker chipping away at my frazzled mind, the thought jabs me until I realize—Lizzie is condemned. In the eyes of the community, she is a witch. Without a trial. Without honest evidence. She is convicted. I have been to other trials, after all. I have seen the travesties of justice with my own eyes.

My bones quiver as though intent on breaking through my skin. My hands pick at my hair, my cheeks. My mouth opens but no sound comes forth. I can no longer live like this.

The sun drops behind clouds, and with the thickening darkness my vexation increases. Shadows creep toward me, one by one, inch by inch, their tenebrous fingers heckling me, revealing in vivid detail how Lizzie suffers right now, in this very moment, in the squalor of the dungeon, chained to the wall, with slithers of straw to sleep on and barely enough food to eat or water to drink. Look here, the wicked shadows say. Here is how she suffers now. And she will suffer still more in the end, her and the babe. I wave my hands desperately before my face, trying to erase the oncoming obscurity and the plodding shadows with it.

Again, I pick at myself, my coat, my eyebrows, my earlobes. Pick. Pick. Pick. Then I pace. Between the picking and the pacing I feel Sanity loosening its grip on me. I have enough sense left to realize how others cross the road to escape the sight of me. I must stop this, I know, but I pace, and I pick, and a crowd gathers.

"Ain't that Wentworth the Younger?" asks a man, a farmer, I think.

Another man answers. "What's it to you?"

I feel Lizzie so fully then. She is suffering on the other side of that wall, so close to me, yet I cannot help her. I am certain that I can hear her strained breathing and the sound drives me mad.

"Stop!" I yell at the onlookers. "What do you stare at? My wife is in there! Innocent people suffer in there!" I point at the prison wall. "Have you no eyes to see their suffering? No ears to hear their cries in the night? And what do any of you do but leer and point and laugh? What have you done to help them? How can you stand there like everything is fine when this madness has overtaken Salem!" I charge toward the farmer, and since I am a head taller than him he backs away.

"James." Father grasps my shoulder, his small eyes narrowing with concern. His gentle voice soothes me. "Son, you cannot do this. People already whisper about how you must be bewitched yourself. You cannot help Lizzie from inside there." He jabs his elbow toward the prison.

I nod at the wall. "I love you, Lizzie," I say. "I will see you soon." Father takes my shoulder and leads me away. For that moment, at least, I leave the shadows behind.

CHAPTER 1

James Wentworth's arms jutted toward the ceiling, grasping upward. Long-form shadows like grasping claws inched toward him and he bolted upright in bed. His heart slammed against his ribcage like a clenched fist. He opened his eyes and sat up, his breathing a fish-like gasp for air.

When James was awake enough to think clearly, the red-hot anger from his dream shook him with its ferociousness. He wanted to strangle the shadows that insisted on creeping toward him, even now when he was awake. Even the realization that he was not in Salem, and it was not the seventeenth century, didn't help him feel better. The fact that he was in his own bed in his own house with his wife asleep by his side didn't help either. The leers of the passers-by still cut into him, their accusations echoing in his ears. He opened his mouth, ready to scream at them to stop staring, until wispy streams of moonlight illuminated his wife sleeping peacefully beside him, a soft smile on her lips. James watched her until his breathing settled.

"Sarah is all right," he whispered. "Sarah is all right." He kept repeating the phrase as if to remind himself that he was not there, in the frightening world of his nightmare, but here.

Quietly, not wishing to disturb her, he crawled out of bed. He slipped his bathrobe over his pajamas and pulled on some socks. He checked the children's room and both were fine, sleeping calmly, Gracie in her bed with her stuffed teddy beside her, Johnny in his crib, his cherubic face peaceful in repose. James smiled at his children, still amazed by them, and he left them to rest.

He opened the front door and let the cool ocean air wash over him. He shivered but didn't go back inside. Something about the snappy air soothed him, reminding him that he was alive, like any other human. And he needed the reminder then. That he was human.

It had been one year since James, Sarah, and Grace moved from Massachusetts to California for his position in the English department at UC Berkeley. It had been an odd year, certainly. It wasn't simply a move from the east coast to the west coast. It wasn't simply taking a new professorship at a new university. He had changed positions more times than he could count. The true test was coming to terms with his mortality again.

For James had spent more than three centuries as a preternatural man. Even he had to remind himself that it was true. He was turned into a vampire in 1692, and since then, he had spent each of his waking nights dreaming of being human again. He had never asked to be a vampire, after all. The vampire who turned him didn't ask his permission, didn't even know his name. James was chosen, led away in the darkness when the stronger, paranormal man bit into James' neck and sucked out his mortal blood only to be replaced with the mystical variety that brought James extraordinary strength, supernatural abilities, and a lifetime of forever.

Forever.

Humans didn't understand the implications of forever, James thought. They all dream of living forever. They don't understand what they are asking for. Living forever becomes a matter of boredom, of finding ways to fill the time. Living for so long makes it harder to maintain some intention for your life. Goals are meaningless since you have forever to work on them. An eternal life means that you go on after those you love most in the world die. That was the worst of it, for James. His wife had died, his beloved Lizzie, and he was forced to go on. When the opportunity came for him to return to a normal human life, he grabbed it. He was certain that being human again would take all his worries away.

James stood outside, continuing to let the ocean wind soothe him. He shivered again and hugged his arms around his chest. Embracing the cold, he was reminded that now he lived in an easily wounded, all too mortal body with ordinary senses. He ate ordinary food and drank ordinary liquids. But being human again had difficulties he hadn't remembered from the first time. He hadn't been sleeping, which was itself enough to wreak havoc on a human's delicate system.

When he was a vampire, night was when he was awake. Everything happened at night. For a human, night meant slowing down, resting, and then sleep. But James couldn't sleep at night. During how many dark hours had he found himself awake, haunted by horrific visions from a time he was determined to forget? Sometimes, he saw leering grins and accusatory squints. Sometimes, he heard jeering voices and cackling laughter. He would lie awake staring at the ceiling as if it were a movie theater screen while tragedies from his past flickered like an old-time film. Sometimes, the scenes were painful and he covered his eyes with his hands. The shadows haunted him the most. Always the shadows. He could not escape them. Finally, when the visions became too much, he crawled out of bed and inspected the hidden corners, the closet, behind the door. Then he searched near the children until he was certain the apparitions were in his mind and not the house. The more he tried to ignore the shadows, the more haunted he felt.

During the daylight hours, at Berkeley or at home, he managed to smile. He fooled everyone, even himself, into thinking he was fine, just fine. I'm a little tired, he'd say, or I haven't completed my research on Poe and Gothic literature, he'd say. If he couldn't admit his troubles to himself, he certainly couldn't admit them to Sarah. She would want to hear them, comfort him, and help him any way she could. He knew that as certainly as he knew the sun would rise in the east. But she had been through so much already, and he didn't want to add to her troubles. It was his job to protect her, after all. She deserved a peaceful, quiet life full of love and joy, and he would do everything in his power to see that she had that and more.

James could not stop shivering. He nodded when he recalled how cold was all he knew until one year ago. That one fateful night, at the height of the witch hunts in Salem, he had followed that long-faced man with the wicked grin who insisted he could help James rescue his wife from the prison. James, desperate to break his wife free, would have followed the man anywhere, even to an abandoned house in an isolated part of town where James would wake up dead. He was awake, but he was dead. Which is what makes a vampire, James thought.

He had believed, in his naiveté, that returning to human would be the easiest thing in the world, far easier than learning how to live like a vampire. After he had been turned into the stuff of nightmares, he was left completely alone. Whoever turned him had vanished into the moonless night, leaving James to figure out how to live this preternatural lifestyle for himself. It was years of challenging lessons and James had hated every moment of it. He shuddered to think of it now.

It was Miriam, the witch, who helped him learn how to live that unnatural way. Miriam was Olivia Phillips' ancestor, and Olivia was one of James' dearest friends. James had known Olivia's family since the seventeenth century. He remembered the first time he saw Miriam and her sisters in Old Salem at the height of the madness. James closed his eyes, struggling to stay in the present moment. It was all too easy to slip back to colonial times in his mind. He had to force his thoughts to stay there, in his home near the California coast, with his wife and children near him. He laughed aloud when he thought of Olivia's last visit to Berkeley when Olivia, ever motherly, ever patient, was determined to teach him to meditate, with no success.

"I can't quiet my mind, Olivia," James said. "There's more than 300 years of thoughts and memories in there."

"Meditation isn't about quieting the mind, James," Olivia answered, her gold hoop earrings jangling in the shake of her head. "You can't stop your brain from thinking. That's what brains are designed to do: think. The trick isn't stopping your thoughts from occurring, but instead acknowledging them as they come, recognizing them for what they are, just thoughts, and letting them slip away without judgment. Thoughts aren't good or bad. You're the English professor. What's that quote from Shakespeare about things not being good or bad?"

"There is nothing either good or bad, but thinking makes it so. From Hamlet."

"Precisely! Thoughts just are, and we should learn to acknowledge those thoughts without attaching positive or negative emotions to them. Whenever I have a particularly unnerving thought, I imagine it floating away from me on a puffy white cloud across a clear blue sky."

Olivia stopped, leaning close to James, that detective seeking clues look etched deep into her steel gray eyes. When James said nothing, she sighed. "You need to learn to live in the moment, dear. The past is gone and the future is a dream."

They were sitting on a blanket on the sand near the shore watching the sun drop, a mist fanning the waves while birds flittered away in the dusk. For a moment, the Pacific Ocean reminded James of the Atlantic Ocean, and he felt Salem very strongly then.

"I should live in the moment?" James asked. "Which moment would that be?"

"This one. Now. The one where you and I are having this conversation. The one where your wife and children are waiting for you at home. You're holding too much onto the past and it's time to let go."

"When you're my age, Olivia, there's a lot of past to contend with."

"Today you are 31 years old, nearly 32, to be exact. And I do think you would get a lot out of meditating. You should speak to Sarah. Meditation has helped her deal with many of the troubles from her past. It's not the easiest thing in the world to realize that you're the reincarnation of a woman who died tragically during the Salem Witch Trials."

"I know," James said. "I was there." He thought a moment, watching the last flock of seagulls depart. "Sarah is better at letting go than I am. Actually, she's better at everything than I am."

"Yes, dear, I'd say that's true."

Olivia smiled in her warm, motherly way, and James allowed himself to be comforted, for that moment at least. Olivia wouldn't let James return to the house without promising to take five minutes a day to sit quietly with his thoughts. James agreed, mainly so Olivia would drop the subject. He extended his hand to his friend and they walked back to his house.

That night, nearly a month after that conversation, James decided to give meditation a try. How could some deep breathing hurt, after all? He closed his eyes, as Olivia had instructed him. Inhale. Exhale. So far, so good. Every time a thought popped into his mind he didn't fight it. He tried to imagine that cloud. For a moment, he saw it. The clear blue sky. The cotton-like cloud. He pushed one thought toward the cloud, settled it as if putting his baby son in his crib, and sent it on its merry way. He sent away a second thought, and a third. Then it happened, as it always did. Darkness descended like a rancorous thunderstorm. There was nowhere to hide as the shadows crept toward him. He shivered, not from the night ocean wind, but from fear. He thought he'd be frozen in darkness forever.

He opened his eyes, scanning his front yard. It was a clear night sky, not a cloud anywhere, and he breathed more easily. The only shadows he saw were those created by the street lamps. Elongated cars, lopsided houses, even his own form, long and distorted, stretched before him. These were not the nightmarish shadows disturbing his sleep. Instead of fear, he was angry. He had lost so much. His wife had lost so much. He had been consumed by so much grief over so many years.

Where is that anger supposed to go, James wondered? Olivia said you should acknowledge your thoughts without attaching emotion to them. But what if that isn't possible? What if the grief was too much? What if he were weighed down by outrage? What if his anger was righteous?

James waited until his breathing settled before he went back inside. He found his way to the bedroom, crawled into bed beside his wife, snuggling closer to share her warmth, and, finally, he slept.

CHAPTER 2

Sarah Wentworth cracked open the door to the room behind the kitchen that James used as an office. She knew what he meant to be doing. The "publish or perish" part of being a tenure-track professor had started to haunt his presentation to the review board since he hadn't done much by way of research or publication since arriving at Berkeley. Every time they discussed it, the conversation was the same.

"I've been a professor for more than 300 years, Sarah," James would say. "I think I'm finally tired of it. The students are young and getting younger. And what is there for me to research that I haven't written about a thousand times before?"

Every time, Sarah suggested that James should take a sabbatical, or, even more drastic, perhaps it was time to leave being a professor behind. He was right, after all. He had been teaching at various universities around the world since the eighteenth century. Maybe it was time for him to find a new passion, she said. And every time James would shrug, saying, no, it will be all right. I think I've found a new angle from which to tackle Poe, or I have an angle of attack on another professor's Marxist take on Dickinson. I'll weather this burnout as I have in the past—by pushing through until I feel some new excitement for my work again.

So Sarah knew what she would find on the other side of the door. She wouldn't find her husband writing a chapter of the scholarly tome he meant to write about Gothic fiction. She peeked around the door and saw him leaning toward the television on his desk, muttering at the Red Sox game.

"Not winning?" Sarah asked.

"Not fielding the ball, not hitting, not pitching, and not winning." James muttered at the television once more before turning the game off.

Sarah stood behind James and saw the blank page on his laptop. "And not writing."

James shook his head. "And not writing." He glanced out the window, his favorite in the house since it had the clearest view of the coastline. "Actually, I've been thinking of writing something else."

"Focusing on someone besides Poe?"

"Perhaps you're right, Sarah. Perhaps it's time I admit that being a professor no longer suits me. The work is so much harder than it was even 10 years ago, and not in a good way. I've always had to prove my worth as a professor, that's part of the job, but the bureaucracy has become ridiculous. As much as I love to teach, teaching is such a small part of the job now. These days they care more about how much money you can dredge up to fund your own research. They care more about which journals you're published in. They don't seem to care whether or not you're helping students learn, which I always thought was the purpose of a university."

"I know what you mean," Sarah said. "There was a time when I couldn't imagine being anything but a librarian. Now I'm happy at home with the kids."

"Which is an important job, Sarah."

"I know. And I'm lucky I have a husband who understands that." She smiled as he flipped the TV back on, checked the game's score, and muttered again as he turned the volume down. "So what do you want to write if you're not writing for work?"

"I thought I'd write about my life, not as a memoir, of course. I couldn't get away with that."

"Why not? People know of the existence of vampires now. They might be interested to hear the story of someone who used to be undead."

"No. I don't want that kind of attention, for me or for you and the children. I want to write about my story as a way for me to share my experiences. It would be better if I wrote it as a novel, I think."

Sarah was quiet as she considered. Finally, she said, "You know that Olivia thinks you should learn to leave your past behind, James."

"Yes, I know. She's told me enough times. But there's something always there, nagging me. I know you've done such a better job dealing with the past than I have. I can't let it go, Sarah."

Sarah removed James' eyeglasses so she could get a better look into his sky-like eyes. There were centuries of pain behind those eyes, she knew, and it hurt her to see him still suffering.

James smiled in an attempt to lighten the mood. "Olivia still wants me to try to meditate."

"Whenever we've tried it together all you do is complain about how much your back hurts while you're sitting there."

"I'm not used to feeling physical pain, Sarah. I felt no pain at all for more than 300 years." He kissed her hand. "Not physical pain, anyway."

Sarah put her arms around James' neck and pressed her forehead against his. "If you think writing about your life will help, then I think you should do it."

"That will mean I'll have virtually nothing to show the tenure committee when my presentation is due."

"Change is good. I know you came to Berkeley for a change, but maybe the change you need is different than what you thought it would be." She kissed his forehead and walked to the door. She stopped with her hand on the knob and turned to him. "And I don't want you to think that I'm better than you at dealing with everything that happened during the witch hunts. I still have flashbacks from when I was in prison."

"Really?" James sat forward in his chair. "Why didn't you tell me?"

"Because it doesn't happen often and I can shake the sadness away as soon as I feel it. But I do remember things. I remember starving, with barely enough water to drink, and the fetid smells, and being chained to the wall. I remember drifting away until I was gone. And then there I was in this new life. Yes, I remember our previous life, but then I was wherever that place is in the universe where souls wait until it's their turn to be reborn. You've been here all along. And now that you're human again, well, that's a lot of memories for one person to handle."

James reached toward his wife. Sarah stepped close to him and he pressed his lips to Sarah's, lingering there. Sometimes, even a year after returning to human, it was a shock for Sarah when she felt the warmth of James' body pressing against her. She had grown used to him as he was when they were first reunited. She loved him in whatever form he took.

"Have I told you lately how lucky I am to be married to you, Sarah Wentworth? Have I told you how lucky I am to have a wife who knows me so well?"

"Yes, but I don't mind hearing it again."

James kissed Sarah, passionately. They stayed there, glued by their lips, until Johnny called from his crib. Sarah smiled at James and they went together to check on their son.

WHEN SARAH AWOKE the next morning, James was gone. She touched where he slept and felt the cold side of his bed, so he must have left some time ago. It was still early, the sun rising in goldenrod rays filtering through the coastal clouds. Sarah knew how James liked to protect her from his struggles, but she knew it was hard for him to be on a daylight schedule when he had been a night owl for so long. She asked him once if he liked being human again. His words were right: Of course, darling, yes, everything is fine, I love being human again. But she heard the high-pitched strain in his voice, saw the too-wide smile, and she knew. Geoffrey, the vampire who turned James, once offered to turn James back.

"Come now, old boy," Geoffrey said, slapping his hand to his knee during one of his midnight visits. "Don't you miss it? Being indestructible? Being immortal? I would imagine indigestion is a terrible thing. Terrible."

It was a flash, but Sarah saw it, James' pause before he said no, absolutely not, he wouldn't change a thing about his life the way it was.

"I don't want to be a vampire again, Geoffrey. I've told you so many times."

But Sarah understood. Even if James did want to be paranormal again, he wouldn't go through with it because he loved her too much. She wasn't sure what she thought of that. She wanted James to be happy, and she wasn't convinced he was happy as he was. Maybe returning to paranormal was the right choice for James.

Sarah got out of bed, pulled her robe over her thin nightgown, and checked on the children. She didn't want to miss a moment as they grew. If her life had taught her anything it was to never take anything for granted, especially her family.

It was early, so Sarah let the children sleep and she went into the kitchen to make some coffee. When James returned, she saw him, still tall, still blond. No, he wasn't as strong as he had been when he was preternatural, but he was as strong as he needed to be. She loved him no matter what he was, human, supernatural, or otherwise. No matter what, he was her James.

She took one look at his strained features and understood that it was more than his morning run that was bothering him. He went on his run every morning, first because he had to work to stay in shape now, and second because he had to release the pent-up energy that kept him awake nights.

"Can I help?" she asked. She refilled his water bottle and waited while he finished it in two gulps. James wiped the water from his lips and shook his head.

"It's nothing."

"It's me you're talking to. What's wrong?"

James wandered into the living room and petted the tailless black cat sleeping on the back of the sofa. He said nothing for a while, but Sarah waited, knowing that it took him some time to get the words straight in his head. It's the English professor in him, she thought. He likes his words to be perfect before anyone hears them, even me. She touched his arm, and he looked at her in surprise, as though he had forgotten she was there.

"I had a dream last night," he said. "About Salem. In the old days."

"What are you dreaming about?"

"About..." He shook his head, not wanting to continue.

"James, I was there. You can say it. You dreamed of when I was in prison."

James laughed. "You're becoming more like Olivia every day with your mind reading."

"The only mind I can read is yours. You dreamed about when I was in prison and?"

"It's been the same dream for weeks. People walking along the streets are cajoling me while I sit outside the prison walls. Some are ready to accuse me of witchcraft. I can feel you slipping away from me behind that prison wall. All I wanted was to escape with you. Father and I were making our plans. We were going to break you out. We were working with some pirate Father knew."

"A pirate! How romantic."

"It's not a joke, Sarah." James stilled himself. "I'm sorry. Of course you know it's not a joke. I'm still getting used to human dreaming, I guess. I didn't dream all those years when I was turned, or I don't think I did. But whether I'm normal or paranormal, the memories of the witch hunts are always there, whether I'm sleeping or awake. I feel like the people from that time are ready to reach out and rattle me until I haven't any sense left."

Sarah gestured to the sofa, and James sat, his hands on his knees, his head bowed.

"Do you remember when I first arrived in Salem and I was haunted by my memories from the witch trials?" Sarah asked.

"Of course," James said.

"I learned to deal with the nightmares by keeping a journal. Every time I woke up with a dream, whether it was good or bad, I wrote it down. Of course, I couldn't make sense of them on my own. I thought I was dreaming about my ancestor who lived in Salem during the witch trials. Olivia and Martha helped me realize I was that ancestor —I am Elizabeth."

"You think I should keep a journal?"

"Why not? You've been keeping journals for as long as I've known you. Maybe if you write your dreams down you'll be able to make sense of them."

"Perhaps."

"You could ask Olivia to take a look at your journal once you have some dreams written down. She looked at my dream journal and she helped me more than you could ever understand."

"Oh, I understand. Olivia has done a lot for me too."

Sarah smiled, remembering James' return. "Of course. She loves you like family. She'd want to help however she could."

James looked outside, saw the bright sun lighting the coastline, and he knew Sarah was right. He had to make sense of the images haunting his sleep. And Olivia was the one who could help.

CHAPTER 3

That afternoon, James stopped by the bookstore on the campus of UC Berkeley. He had some time before his next class. A walk across the green grounds under the bright blue sky always cheered him, even if the sun still hurt his eyes. He pulled out his dark sunglasses and they helped, some. Still, he found the glowing sunbeams heartening. They made the shadows around him, his own and everywhere around him, less formidable.

In the space of a breath, James was transported back in time, not to the seventeenth century, but to a few years ago. That day in the library in Salem he had seen the sun for the first time in years. In some ways, that time in Salem felt more ancient than Massachusetts during the witch hunts. James and Sarah had only just been reunited after three centuries. Even in Sunny California, James shook with horror at the memories of losing her. He had been empty, longing, waiting for oh so very long. Then fate, or magic, or both, brought his Lizzie home to him in the form of his Sarah.

He smiled when he remembered how unsure she was of him at first. Of course, he knew her from the moment he saw her standing outside his house. She had been drawn to their wooden gabled home because somewhere inside she knew she belonged there. And at the time he was, well, not human, and she had every right to be wary. In time, with patience, she was in his arms again, and for a brief moment all was right with the world.

That damned reporter. Even now James' fists clenched at the memory of Kenneth Hempel, the man who dedicated his life to ridding the earth of the undead. To save Sarah, James decided to beat Hempel at his own game. James went outside in the sun to show the reporter that he, James, was not what he truly was—a vampire. How James survived the ordeal, he still didn't know. The memory of that moment was too much. James stopped, eyes closed, straining to hear the students walking past, talking, laughing, and he remembered that his hearing was not what it used to be. He opened his eyes, and though the sun was bright, it was no longer deadly to him, and perhaps, he thought, scolding himself, he should remember that. The past was always there, though. He was certain he would never escape it.

James forced himself to remain still, feeling the sun on his face, his neck, his hands, and he noticed once again how much brighter, happier things looked during the day. Sarah had told him about research that showed how sunlight is good for you, mainly because of the Vitamin D, but there were other health and emotional benefits as well.

"I wouldn't be surprised if you have seasonal affective disorder with the lack of sunlight you've had," Sarah said.

"We live in California, one of the sunniest places in the world," James answered.

"Having no sunlight for centuries must have some cumulative effect."

James opened his eyes and stood there in the full light of the sun, dark glasses off, his arms outstretched as he soaked in the light. He admitted to himself, if only grudgingly, that he did feel better.

He began to feel a bit obvious as a few students smiled at him as they walked past. He went into the bookstore, past the racks of UC

Berkeley hoodies and baseball caps, past the textbooks, and past the display of recently published books by Berkeley professors. James shook his head, thinking he had been a fool for neglecting his academic work for so long. He would have nothing to show for his time at Berkeley except a few articles in not quite exceptional journals and a half-finished book about Poe. And that was it. Forget writing about his dreams, he thought. He'd have to look for some other job soon enough.

He wandered to the aisle with the bound journals and spiral notebooks. He picked up a black and white spotted composition book and turned it over in his hands. He was reminded of Sarah's dream journal and decided why not? It certainly couldn't hurt to keep track of his dreams. He didn't need anything fancy for his journal and this would do. He paid at the front of the store, dropped it into his black backpack, and headed toward class. At least he still enjoyed teaching, though the tenure committee didn't care much about actually teaching anyone anything. Really, he would rather not have any more nightmares about Old Salem. He was tired of the frightful visions, but he knew his dreams were not done with him.

LATER THAT EVENING, when James arrived home, he found Sarah and the children on the living room floor playing with blocks with letters on them. More worries prickled him, as if a ferocious lion leapt toward his family, and he saw Sarah and the children swiped away as suddenly as Lizzie and Grace had been torn from him. Just like that, with the snap of two fingers, and those fingers pointing accusations, and those accusations spreading like a pebble dropped in a pond, and those rings spreading wider until they were too far to see, and suddenly no one in Salem was safe.

Sarah could not take her eyes from her husband's face. She reached for his hand and smiled. James felt his muscles relax and his worries melt away. Sarah's touch was enough to settle him. He recalled Olivia saying that all lives had their difficulties. Every person born, past, present, or future, has their own stories and their own struggles. There is no one who doesn't have some obstacle they must face, and it's sheer arrogance to think that we will live only a charmed life.

James could think of nowhere he would rather be than beside his family at that moment. He sat on the floor near Sarah, and Grace watched with rapt awe as he built a tower with the blocks. James kissed the top of his daughter's gold curls. He wanted desperately to believe that he had already had so many problems in his long life that he had used up his obstacles for this lifetime, if there was another life to come. He felt like a cat that had used its nine lives and there was nothing left after this. He watched Johnny bounce while Sarah knocked the tower down so they could begin again.

Johnny was six months old already. James and Sarah often commented on what a good baby he was–quiet, even-tempered, curious. So much like his mother. Johnny had Sarah's dark hair and James' blue eyes, and when James looked at his son he saw the image of his wife, which made him happy. Grace looked more like him, he knew. That's how he and Sarah knew they had found her again after more than 300 years. Like most fathers, he was certain that both of his children looked like angels: Johnny, with his sweet face and cherub cheeks, Grace with her kind eyes and gentle smile. James knew how lucky he was. He had no life for so long—literally, no life. He had been dead, without breathing, without heartbeat, and he lived as if he were dead. Yes, he walked, and he talked, and he taught his classes, but that was all. He existed. Now he had his little family. Remembering his purchase at the campus bookstore, James realized that this here, this family, was reason enough to try Sarah's idea of writing down his nightmares.

Yet even there, on the floor with his family, his wife glowing, his children laughing, the shadows of the past reached for him as though determined to pull him away. James went into the kitchen to pour himself a glass of water. He struggled to put the visions of Puritan madness aside, and he grew angry with himself for his inability to do so.

He listened to Sarah play with the children and struggled to focus on the uplifting sounds of their voices. But, no, he was in Salem again, watching his beloved father's maid turn on them when they weren't sufficiently impressed with the afflicted girls' performance. James and his father had been in the Meeting House when the accused were questioned by the magistrates as though those wicked girls could do no wrong. He listened as neighbor turned on neighbor seeking attention for themselves.

And what had James done to stop the madness? He spent years brimming with anger at the people of Old Salem for their willingness to participate in the havoc. And then it was too late. Their quiet lives became violent. Innocent people were arrested and hanged. His Lizzie died in prison. He would have been arrested too if Geoffrey, with his preternatural plans, hadn't stepped in.

Even if the witch hunts had begun as a joke, at some point the situation became dangerous. Yet it continued. And James blamed everyone. But what had he done? He remembered his plan, his and his father's, to break Elizabeth out of prison. But was that enough? He had watched his whole world go mad while he stood on the sidelines. He was amused by it at first, then concerned as he saw respected people like Rebecca Nurse arrested, but he never spoke out. He never tried to talk sense into anyone. That is, not until after Lizzie was arrested.

He saw Sarah's worried glances in his direction, but he stayed in the kitchen, giving himself time to think about what he should say to her. Now he was having waking dreams, which were more dangerous, he knew. He wanted to talk to Sarah about it, but she was busy with the children and he didn't want to interrupt their playtime with his foolish worries. Hadn't Grace suffered enough? Was she even cognizant of what happened to her? After all, she hadn't been born yet when she died. Perhaps she didn't know. At least, this is what James hoped.

He knew what Sarah would say about his meandering thoughts: people wouldn't listen to reason then. Even Increase Mather, one of the most respected preachers of the day, couldn't get the citizens of Salem to listen. Witch hunts were as common as mouse traps then—a way to rid the community of the pestilence of witchcraft. In 1692, the madness had taken on a life of its own. Maybe James' speaking out wouldn't have helped. He realized, with a breathlessness like a sucker punch to his gut, that he had been as much a part of the problem as anyone for staying silent.

He should have been more courageous. He should have spoken his mind instead of gawping at the trials like a spectator at an afternoon's entertainment. He did nothing until it was too late. He didn't care until his wife, his own heart, was arrested. He saw the accusations and the unfairness everywhere, yet he did nothing.

Later that night, alone in their room, Sarah took his hand in hers and held it close to her heart.

"James."

He said nothing.

She said the words he knew were coming. He knew her so well.

"I know you're still struggling about Salem. We've had this conversation so many times. Are you not hearing me?"

"I hear you, my love. But I'm not sure I believe you."

Sarah sighed. She shivered when an ocean breeze pressed icy air through the open window. She wrapped her bathrobe around her shoulders and pulled the window shut. When she still shivered, James wrapped his arms around her and pulled her close. She exhaled, pressing herself closer into his chest.

"I love that you're warm now," she said. James remained quiet, still unsure what to say.

"James, when I was arrested you were outside that jail every day begging anyone you could find to help me. You had no concern for your own safety and you were so close to being arrested yourself. You were braver than other people then, most of whom stayed away even after someone they loved was arrested. Please, you have to stop blaming yourself. You have to come to terms with what happened, and you need to accept that you did the best you could under the circumstances. Sometimes, things spiral too far out of control and we have to manage things the best we can. That's all anyone can do when the situation becomes hard."

James nodded. He knew Sarah was right, but he couldn't stop feeling like he was no better than anyone else. He let the madness go on while he acted like an ostrich with his head in the sand. Or like Johnny playing peek-a-boo. He didn't know if he could ever forgive himself.

CHAPTER 4

James' birthday, the nineteenth of April, approached quickly, though he paid little attention. Sarah decided that his birthday was something to celebrate so she arranged for everyone important to them to come to Berkeley. This was only his second birthday in over 300 years after all. He was now, he laughed to think, the ripe old age of 32.

Olivia arrived a few days early to spend quality time with her favorite Wentworths, as she liked to say. When she climbed out of the Honda Uber, James marveled at how Olivia always looked the same. Her sympathetic motherly expression flashed a warm smile in his direction. She still looked ever the gypsy in her wide-sleeved white blouse and her flowing peasant skirt, her large hoop earrings dancing in the wind.

It was always a family holiday when Olivia visited. She brought gifts for the children from her Wiccan shop in Salem, the Witches Lair. She had a good-luck bracelet for Grace and tarot blocks for Johnny. She brought plenty of hugs and kisses too. Olivia thought of Grace and Johnny as her grandchildren though they weren't blood related. That hardly mattered to Olivia. James had known Olivia's family for so long, and as far as she was concerned he was family. She had always thought of James as a son even though he was older than her by about three centuries.

The day after her arrival, while Sarah was out and the children were sleeping, James and Olivia sat on the patio under the wide umbrellas blocking the sun. Olivia leaned back in the lawn chair, her wide sunglasses protecting her eyes. She looked relaxed, as though she were visiting a spa.

"Enjoying California?" James asked.

"I always enjoy California, dear. I've been thinking about selling the Witches Lair and moving here permanently."

"I can't imagine it. Olivia Phillips without the Witches Lair?" James shook his head at the thought. "What would you do without Salem?"

"The same thing I do with it. Live my life. Enjoy my family and friends."

"I thought you'd want to move to Oklahoma after Jennifer and Chandresh adopted the baby."

"Of course, I would love that, but I don't think Jennifer would be too keen on the idea. You know how she always thinks I'm meddling even though I'm only trying to help. I have the distinct impression that Jennifer is perfectly happy living across the country from me."

James nodded. He poured Olivia a fresh glass of iced tea and realized that Olivia was the closest thing to a mother he had. His own mother died when he was 27. He had been 27 in 1689.

Olivia looked toward the driveway and laughed when she saw James' car.

"I see you're still driving the same Ford Explorer. I'm surprised you didn't buy something new with all the other changes you've gone through."

Her emphasis on the word *changes* made James smile. "I like the car. It runs perfectly fine. Why change what works?"

"I could have said the same to you. You know, James, I don't know if I can ever forgive you for what you put me through when I returned you to human. I never knew being a witch could be so hard."

"You were perfect that night, Olivia. So was Martha. It's what I wanted, and I'll always be thankful to you for doing it even though you didn't want to."

"Didn't want to? I was terrified! Returning vampires to humans has been done so rarely, and not always with the best results. I didn't want to accidentally kill you."

"I was already dead, Olivia."

Olivia pulled her lips into a flat line. She exhaled as she watched seagulls float overhead.

"No," she said finally. "I'm not having this discussion with you again." She closed her eyes, again in resort spa mode. Finally, she asked, "How are you, James? Really. Those nightmares...?"

"I'm fine, Olivia."

She squinted at him. "Are you? I seem to recall a conversation we had on your front lawn."

James squinted into the distance. "I'm fine, Olivia."

"I don't believe you. I can see that you're still uncomfortable in your human body. The way you're hunching your shoulders. The way you're avoiding looking directly at me. Did we make the right decision, James? Are you happy being human again? Are you upset that I returned you? Sarah said you paused when Geoffrey offered to turn you again."

"She noticed that, huh?"

"Sarah knows you better than she knows herself." Olivia sipped her iced tea without taking her eyes from James, her detective seeking clues look at full force. "There's nothing to be ashamed of if you're still struggling. It's only been a year since you've been returned. You were paranormal for so long, and maybe living a human life isn't all you remembered it to be."

James reached across the patio table and took Olivia's hand. "I'm very happy being human, Olivia. I don't mind being mortal. Sarah and I should be the same. I've always felt that."

"Then what's troubling you?"

James knew better than to deny his feelings to Olivia any longer. She was Olivia, the most intuitive person he knew, as well as one of the most powerful witches in the world. Only a witch wielding great powers could pull off the spell that returned vampire James into a human being. She knew something was bothering him, so he might as well tell her the truth.

"Yes, it's the nightmares. Only they're not nightmares anymore. They're waking dreams now, and they're terrifying me."

"Something has changed. What has changed, and why is it bothering you?"

"It's more than just remembering Old Salem. Now I'm overwhelmed with memories about how little I did to stop the madness."

"Have you told Sarah?"

"She knows."

"And what did she have to say?"

"There was nothing more I could have done."

"You ought to try listening to your wife more often, James. It would save you a lot of heartache." It was Olivia's turn to reach for James. "It's human nature to ignore a problem until it touches them. We see problems around us every day. We know about poverty, the environment, violence. We see people behaving badly and we do nothing, or we allow ourselves to be entertained by it, and by the time it touches us or someone we love it's too late—the situation has escalated and the common person can no longer stop it. But even the worst in Old Salem stopped. The madness did end."

"Not until people suffered and died."

"Sometimes it takes a tragedy to get people to wake up. But you and Sarah have a new life here. You have two beautiful children, including the Grace you were missing. You have a great position at a wonderful university, and Sarah is happy being home with Grace and Johnny. You have a beautiful home by the shore. It's almost as pretty as Salem. Almost."

James laughed. "And you were thinking of leaving Salem?"

"Sometimes I think I need a change of scenery, to experience somewhere new, but then I think of Salem, think of the seaside, think of the history, good and bad, and I know my family has been there since the time of the witch hunts...well, you know our story. So you're right. I'll never leave Salem, at least not permanently. Right now it's enough for me that I get to come visit you and Sarah and the children, and I get to go to Oklahoma to visit Jennifer and Chandresh and little Eric, but then I'm always happy to go home where I belong." Olivia turned her detective stare onto James again. "You're still such an enigma. I was hoping now that you're human again I'd have an easier time understanding you. Yet here you are, just as stone-faced, just as recalcitrant as ever. You don't have any great secret to hide anymore, James. I know why you were so guarded before. You were afraid of letting down your defenses because you couldn't let anyone see the real you. You weren't human at the time, and your instincts were correct—people did respond badly when they discovered that vampires exist. But you're back. You've returned. You have nothing to hide anymore." She looked over the whitewashed fence and saw the coast, the vast blue ocean, the silver-rimmed foam of the waves, the people lounging on the sand or swimming in the water, enjoying the day. "The sun is definitely out more in California," Olivia said.

James followed Olivia's gaze toward the water swimming for the horizon.

"Are you happy here?" Olivia asked.

"I like it well enough. But I miss New England." James shrugged, turning away from Olivia. He felt embarrassed somehow. "I hardly know why. Salem is a place of such sadness for me."

"But it's also a place of great joy. You met Elizabeth in Salem, and you and Sarah were reunited in Salem. You fell in love again in Salem. And you found Grace in Salem. I returned you in Salem. You've always had a tendency to focus on the negative to the exclusion of everything positive. You have to remember the good things that happened too."

"I know I always focus on the bad."

"It's time to stop that. Everything that has happened to you helped to lead you to where you are today. And your life looks pretty good from where I'm sitting. You've never properly dealt with the tragedies in Old Salem, James. You were turned while Elizabeth was imprisoned so you were dealing with the fear of your new preternatural life while dealing with Elizabeth's death. Then you had to live a life on the run like some criminal." Olivia nodded as though she found the answer to the question she had been skirting around.

"I'm not sure there's anything that can be done about it, Olivia. I'm going to have to learn to live with it."

"I don't agree. I think you need to do something about this. You're human again. That means you won't be alive forever. You'll have a human life, with illnesses, and aging. No human knows how long they have. You need to focus all your energy on your family, enjoying each other for however long you're together."

"You're quite a downer today, Miss Olivia."

"I'm being honest. You've carried this around long enough. I think you need to return to Salem. Not permanently. But long enough to make peace with everything that happened. I want to do a reading on you. I want to see if ghosts from that time are haunting you."

"I'm not so sure..."

"Sarah's been through it twice now. She'll tell you about it."

"I don't know, Olivia."

"You trusted me with your life when you allowed me to perform the returning spell on you. You won't let me do a simple reading on you?" She squinted, looking like a strict schoolmarm. "The only reason you wouldn't want to go through with it is if you don't want to learn what I might be able to tell you."

"What might you be able to tell me?"

"What is happening to you. Why the past continues to haunt you. Why you're not able to move on despite the fact that you've regained everything you lost from that time. Why now, after you've been human for a year, are memories of Old Salem bombarding you?"

James sighed. He knew Olivia was right. "So what do we do?"

"I would hypnotize you as I did Sarah and let the spirits speak through me. That's how Sarah was able to speak to your father while you were in Camp Dracula. John spoke through me."

"And the spirits answer your questions?"

"Sometimes. Not always. Spirits work in their own ways in their own time. When I do connect with the other world the answers they give are not always clear. I had the secret to you and Sarah as soon as I did that first reading on Sarah after she arrived in Salem."

"But you had no idea what it meant at the time and we still had to go through that whole ordeal to rediscover each other."

"Was it an ordeal?" Olivia squinted again and James felt as he did when he was a student at Cambridge in the seventeenth century—the all-knowing tutor was about to cut him down to size. "What if that's what you had to go through to find each other? What if it wasn't a waste of time at all but instead it was the universe righting itself for you and Sarah after such a long separation? What if I had been able to say to Sarah outright, 'You're the reincarnation of a woman from the seventeenth century and the man you were married to then is still alive. He still loves you and wants you back.' Do you think Sarah would have believed me? Do you think she would have been able to understand the paranormal world at that time?"

"I understand."

A cry called through the open screen door and James knew that Grace and Johnny had woken from their naps. He and Olivia found their way to the children's room where Grace was sitting up in her bed while Johnny watched wide-eyed from his crib.

Olivia picked Grace up and raised the little girl above her head. Grace squealed with delight.

"Hello, dear! Give Grandma Olivia a kiss." Grace was happy to oblige. "My beautiful Gracie. How big you are!"

James held Johnny in one arm as he embraced Olivia with the other. "I'm glad you're here."

"You know I'm always happy when I can come see you. But I think it's your turn to visit me. You have some unfinished business in Salem to see to."

When Sarah walked into the room James smiled at her with a lightness he hadn't felt in some time. Sarah kissed his cheek, then stepped back to get a better look at her husband.

"What's this?" she asked. She turned to Olivia. "What have you said to him?"

"Nothing he didn't need to hear."

Olivia walked into the living room and extended her arms toward the ceiling. "I love coming to this house. It's so spacious. That ceiling looks like it's tall enough to touch the clouds."

Sarah nodded. "I love this house."

James put Grace into the playpen while Sarah took Johnny into her arms. "More than our house in Salem?" he asked.

"Not more, but in a different way. Our house in Salem is our past. This house is our future."

Olivia winked at James. "Well said, Sarah. We have to put the past behind us so we can look forward strong and unafraid."

Sarah looked from James to Olivia. "Has something happened?"

"I told James I want to do a reading on him."

Sarah laughed. "And what did he say?"

Olivia turned to James. "So are we doing this reading, James Wentworth?"

James looked at Sarah for help, but she shook her head. "If Olivia thinks you need a reading, then you need a reading. I always trust Olivia's instincts."

When he realized that Sarah and Olivia were on the same side, he knew he didn't have a chance. It was easier to give in now.

Olivia looked at the calendar on the kitchen wall. "There's a full moon on Friday night. We should do it during the full moon. I always have better results then."

"Very well," James said. "During the full moon."

He looked at Johnny, who was playing with a lock of Sarah's dark curls, and he looked at Grace, with her arms up wanting out of the playpen. He lifted his daughter, hugged her close, and hoped this reading was the right thing to do.

CHAPTER 5

Two days later it was indeed a full moon. James watched the glowing orb rising overhead and he felt an inkling of sadness. He remembered all those years when he only had the moon and the stars to light his life. He realized that he had hardly ever looked up during the night to see the sky.

Certainly, he and Sarah spent many romantic evenings sitting in their backyard with a bottle of wine and the soft glow of the lanterns after the children had gone to bed. They were simply listening to the lapping waves at low tide, holding hands, talking about their days or books they were reading, sometimes sitting in silence. James could not get enough of staring at Sarah, still marveling at her presence.

The night of the full moon James forced himself to look up. When he was a paranormal man he had been forced by circumstances to lurk in the shadows with burglars and other bandits. Had he been happy then? James didn't know. No, that's not true, he did know. After carrying the pain of Elizabeth's loss for decades he grew numb. He lived the best he could, as close to humans as he could. He still sought the one human goal he could achieve and became a professor and taught at universities around the world. He helped others where he could. But had he been happy? Only when he recalled Elizabeth. Only when he wrote his long letters to her. Perhaps somewhere, deep inside, he knew he would find her again. Or at least he hoped he would. Otherwise, he felt nothing.

Sarah stood behind him. She slipped her arms around his waist and rested her head against his back. "You're looking at the moon. You haven't done that...well, you've never done that, not since I've known you."

"Is there anything that escapes your attention?" James asked. "Even when we were in Salem the first time you knew what I was thinking before I recognized it myself."

"It's about time you noticed."

Sarah let go of James. She looked into the sky, following his gaze. "Are you worried about the reading?"

"Should I be? You've been through it before."

"There's nothing to worry about. It feels a little strange when Olivia goes into her trance. I felt like I was in a trance too, like I was asleep and awake at the same time. But there's nothing frightening about it. Olivia speaks nonsense, or at least it sounds like nonsense at the time."

James sighed. "I don't see how the reading is going to help. I don't know what I need to learn. When you first arrived in Salem you needed to learn who you were, and who I was. But I know you, and I have you, and I don't need anything else."

"We both know that's not true. Something is haunting you, something from our past, and you need to figure out what it is."

Olivia came out of the guest bedroom and joined them in the backyard. James saw her reflection in the glass door as she walked toward them.

"I agree with Sarah," Olivia said.

"Of course you do," James said.

"What do you think he needs to learn?" Sarah asked.

"I think he's being a typical man and not facing his feelings. I think James has a lot of repressed emotions regarding your shared past, and I think he has a lot of residual anger from the witch hunts. He never really faced any of that."

James' face grew hot. "How can you say I never faced any of that? I mourned Elizabeth every day for over 300 years!"

"I don't mean you didn't miss her, dear. Of course, I know you did. But after she died you were on your own for three centuries, and while you mourned her, you never dealt with your anger, as evidenced by your red cheeks right now. You need to examine your frustration with the event itself and your reaction to it. This reading is necessary, James. You never know what you're going to learn from a reading."

"Are you looking for anything specific?" Sarah asked. "For me, it was trying to figure out what my dreams meant. But what about James?"

"Well, James is also having nightmares about the witch trials."

"But I know my dreams are about the witch trials," James said, "which Sarah didn't when she first moved to Salem."

"But you don't know why you're having them *now*." Olivia patted James' hand. "What do you say, Doctor Wentworth? Can we start your reading? It's past midnight and the full moon will begin to wane."

"Very well," James said. "Let's see what happens."

Olivia led James to the dining room table. She darkened all the lights and closed the curtains so the room was black. She lit four white taper candles and set one along the walls in each direction, north, south, east, and west, the flickering gold the only glow in the room. She pulled a chair away from the table. "Come sit, James. Relax. If you're tense or worried the reading may not be clear. I need a direct line from you to the universe in order to hear what the spirits have to tell me."

"Should I leave?" Sarah asked.

"You're welcome to stay as far as I'm concerned," Olivia said. "But really it's up to James."

James pulled out a chair for Sarah. "Of course you can stay. Maybe you can help me make sense of what Olivia says."

"That's a wonderful idea," said Olivia. "I never can remember what I say when I go into a trance, and I think you'd be a great help, Sarah."

Sarah sat next to James. She stroked his arm and kissed his temple. "You'll be fine."

"Do I need to do something?" he asked.

"Olivia does everything," Sarah said. "You just need to sit there and try to clear your mind as much as you can."

"I've never been very good at that."

"Just relax, James," Olivia said. "That's all I need from you. Let's join hands, the three of us."

James, Sarah, and Olivia held hands across the table. Olivia closed her eyes, and James wanted to laugh. The scene reminded him of a movie where the psychic is fake and gives ordinary proclamations that anyone could come up with if they were slightly good at reading people and able to listen to clues people inadvertently shared. Olivia began shaking as though she were on a boat in a turbulent sea, and James stared.

"Yes," Olivia said, her voice sounding far away. "I am beginning to see. They are here. They want to tell you."

"Who is here?" James asked.

"They are. The ones you knew."

"What do they want?" James asked.

"They want you to know. They want you to see. Elizabeth. It was never Elizabeth."

James nearly stopped breathing. "Who did? Who said it was never Elizabeth?"

"Mercy. They ask mercy. And Elizabeth died."

James tried to stand, but Sarah's hand on his arm settled him. He leaned back into his chair and it took some control for him not to shake Olivia out of her trance. He closed his eyes, exhaled, and waited. Sarah smiled at him, and he felt better. He always drew strength from Sarah.

Olivia's eyes fluttered behind her eyelids as though she were in REM sleep. Her whole body shuddered and she opened her eyes. "So? Did I say anything helpful?"

"That's it?" James shook his head and pulled his hand from Olivia. "There's nothing else? What did any of that mean, anyway?"

"There wasn't much," Sarah told Olivia. "You told him that they wanted to tell him something, but you didn't say who they were. They said it was never Elizabeth, and then they said they ask mercy. And that was it."

"Oh, dear," Olivia said. "That doesn't sound very helpful."

"You mentioned that Elizabeth died," James said.

"I'm sorry, James. I wish I could remember what I say when I'm with the spirits. Whatever I do say makes sense in time. You need to keep an open mind because there is a message in there you need to receive."

"Okay, so let's think," James said. "Mercy?"

Sarah nodded. "Mercy Lewis. But we didn't know her. We saw her in the Village a few times, but we never met her. Maybe it didn't mean a name. Maybe it meant forgiveness."

James paced the dining room while Sarah and Olivia watched. He felt their eyes on him, but he needed to keep moving.

"Don't press yourself too hard trying to figure it out tonight," Olivia said. "Sometimes it takes a while to figure out what it means. Right, Sarah?"

"That's right. But then suddenly one day it makes sense and you realize you should have recognized the message from the beginning."

James nodded. But that wasn't enough. He wanted answers, and he was never as patient as Sarah.

Sarah waited for James while he brushed his teeth. He pulled back the quilt and got into bed beside her. "What did you think about the reading?" she asked.

"I think it was pointless."

"We'll figure it out. Tomorrow we'll look up Mercy Lewis. It can still be hard for me to remember specific details from Old Salem, but I think she was a major player in the witch hunts. She was part of the accusations."

"Yes, I…" And then James thought he knew. "Oh, my God, Sarah. Was she the one who accused you of being a witch?"

Sarah closed her eyes. "No, I thought…wasn't it…?" When she opened her eyes she looked far away, as though she had retreated to the seventeenth century. "I believe it was my sister-in-law. I seem to remember her coming to dinner with my brother." She snapped her fingers as if trying to jolt her memory awake.

"Mercy Lewis may not have directly accused you, but she perhaps corroborated the accusation."

"Maybe." Sarah looked toward the door as though expecting someone to appear. "I remember Prudence, your father's housemaid. She was quite taken with you, as I recall, and she wasn't happy that you were no longer on the market. Maybe she had something to do with the accusations too."

"When I chose you for my wife, Prudence became cold, very cold. She was rude to me and stopped listening to Father. Finally, Father had to let her go. I had forgotten all this."

Sarah grabbed James' arm. "I'm certain it was my sister-in-law who accused me. I remember when she first married my brother she couldn't stop putting me down every chance she had. I was talking about a book you read to me, a history of the British monarchy, and I shared something I learned. That woman looked at me and said, as rudely as she could, 'Who knows that sort of thing?' When you said obviously I do, she rolled her eyes and turned away. She always had some kind of sarcastic remark for me, but I said nothing, wanting to keep the family peace. And then she turned on me."

"And cost you your life."

James' expression softened and he even smiled. "I remember that she was one of the ugliest women I've ever seen with her stringy black hair and enough bags under her eyes to take on holiday. She had few accomplishments to her credit where, after you learned how to read, you were better read than most men in those days."

"She felt the lack of something," Sarah said. "Enough to accuse me of witchcraft."

THE NEXT MORNING JAMES' impatience returned. He cornered Olivia in the kitchen while she made tea.

"What do we do now?" he asked.

"This is only the beginning," Olivia said. "There's more behind the story of your nightmares, I can feel it, and until we discover the missing element you'll never be able to leave the past behind."

Sarah appeared carrying a freshly bathed Johnny. James kissed one chubby cheek, and Olivia kissed the other. Olivia paused and looked from James to Sarah and back again. "Were you serious about returning to Salem, James? To face down your fears of the past?"

"Are we returning to Salem?" Sarah asked.

"James has to decide whether or not he's willing to hunt down the demons that are torturing him," Olivia said.

"James." Sarah stood on her toes and looked into her husband's eyes. "We need to go to Salem."

"Very well. I know better than to argue when you've decided on something," James said.

Sarah smiled. "Quite right. By the way, I can't remember if I told you that Grandpa Geoffrey is coming to visit for your birthday."

"Grandpa Geoffrey? Oh, Lord." James nodded at the cup of tea Olivia handed him and took it to the dining room table. The thought of Geoffrey still irked him to no end. "Why did you have to remind me?"

"Because in your heart you love Geoffrey. He's been a good friend to you, and he's learning how to be a grandfather."

James took Johnny from Sarah's arms. He studied the picture of Grace and Johnny on the wall. "Geoffrey does love the children," James said. "All right, so Grandpa Geoffrey is coming. Happy day."

"If I have anything to say about it," Sarah said, "it will be."

CHAPTER 6

James paced his classroom while watching his students. Somehow, the discussion got away from him, as it did sometimes. The energy ran hot or cold. Either the students couldn't be bothered about anything and snuck glances at their phones under their desks or they were all worked up—over what, James wasn't always sure. Somehow, from a discussion about Wuthering Heights, the students had drifted onto women's rights, then onto witch hunts as a means to keep women in line, then on to witch hunts in general. One student started talking about the Salem witch hunts, another student talked about watching The Crucible that weekend, and the rest were involved in their own arguments. James glanced at the clock on the wall, thinking it was better to leave as quickly as he could.

"All right, everyone," he said. "See you next week."

The noon-time sun was high, and James squinted in the bright light piercing the windows. One student raised her hand as she slid her laptop into her backpack. Again, James thought to escape before things got out of control, but old habits remained and he nodded at the young woman.

"Yes?" he asked.

"Do you know anything about what happened in Salem?" she asked.

"Not much," he answered. "Besides, I'm not sure what witch hunts have to do with Wuthering Heights unless you've read a different edition than I have."

"I know we're studying the Brontes now, but I want to know what happened to them all, you know, during the witch hunts in Salem. Was anyone arrested or imprisoned for starting the hysteria?"

Will I never get away from this, James wondered? It would be easier to simply answer her question, he knew. "No one," he said. "Not long after Mather wrote his sermon about how it would be a terrible thing if even one innocent person were hanged, the witch hunts stopped as suddenly as they began. No one was arrested for starting the hysteria. Well," he closed his eyes, the shadows of the past inching toward him in broad daylight. "Tituba, Samuel Parris' slave, was arrested for consorting with the devil. Then all havoc broke loose, and anyone could have been arrested at any time. Salem was a living hell for about six months. And then it stopped." He bounded for the front of the room when he remembered that his backpack was stashed under the lectern. He was determined to make it out of there in one piece. He headed toward the door with long strides.

"But what do the witch hunts mean, Doctor Wentworth? What were they for?"

James stopped with his hand on the doorknob. "I suppose we make meaning from tragedies in a way that helps us understand why things are the way they are now. Today is everyone's responsibility. It's up to each of us to make ourselves heard when we see something that's wrong. Too often we sit back and do nothing when we're not directly affected by the events. We see tragedies on the news and shake our heads and think that's too bad. Sorry not sorry. We allow events to get out of hand until we're personally affected. Then we want to call up armies. But by then it's often too late. If you see something wrong, if you know of something wrong, you have an obligation to speak up. Nothing will ever change as long as we're content to sit back and assume the worst will never happen.

The worst does happen, all too often, as has been evidenced throughout human history. We can't be docile. We can't allow ourselves to be led by others who may not have our best interests at heart."

Another student raised his hand. "What does docile mean?"

James sighed.

"But what if we're going to be in personal danger if we speak out?" the first student asked.

"That's an age-old question, and it's a personal decision," James said. "I believe most people want to help, but they don't, so those who want to do damage can, and often they do that damage for a long time until fate or circumstance stops them. Imagine what a world we'd live in if people followed their instinct to help where they saw it was needed."

It was quiet as the students left. James closed the classroom door and headed to his office. As he walked, he wondered if he had put into words the very issue he had been struggling with himself.

LATER THAT NIGHT, James was at home, at his desk, staring through the window at the ebb and flow of the shapeshifting coastline. He slipped his hand under his shirt, felt his heart beating, and sighed. It had become a daily ritual—checking his own heartbeat, as though he could still hardly believe it was there, as though it could be suddenly taken away from him as quickly as it was given back. This was one of those nights when he missed being awake through the darkness.

He opened his laptop, opened his document, and began typing, attempting to find some new words about Poe and Gothic literature, though he had to admit that he had no new thoughts about either subject since he taught at Eventide College. He heard Grace calling from her room, so he went to his daughter, checked that Johnny was still asleep, and lifted her from her bed.

Grace yawned, and James yawned. Father and daughter retired together to the sofa where they promptly fell asleep. James opened his eyes to the smell of breakfast. He looked at Grace, who was still sleeping, but Johnny was in Sarah's arms as she slipped a tray of coffee and an egg croissant on the side table.

"Thank you, honey," James said. "Aren't you eating?"

"I'm taking Grace and Johnny to daycare," Sarah said. "I promised Leslie I'd help in the library today."

"Old habits." James smiled. "Do you miss working?"

"Sometimes. A bit. But I also like being home with the children. Maybe they'll let me work part-time at the library. It would have to be a flexible schedule though."

James nodded at Grace in his most serious manner. "You're a big girl now who goes to daycare, are you?" Grace laughed and nodded. "And Johnny goes to daycare too?"

"Johnny goes to daycare!" Grace clapped her hands and laughed some more. James never tired of seeing the sparkle in her smile. Sarah's hand reached for their daughter's hair, her fingers gently twisting through the golden curls.

"All right, Grace," Sarah said. "We need to get you dressed so we can leave."

James helped Sarah get the children ready. He opened his arms and pulled his wife toward him. He kissed her, and Sarah pressed her head against his chest.

"I'll see you at Berkeley," she said, and then she leaned in for a quick kiss that James couldn't resist.

"At least it's my Shakespeare seminar, so there shouldn't be any discussions about witches."

"You're not reading Macbeth, are you?"

"Fortunately, no."

Sarah lifted Grace into her arms. "Oh, my goodness, baby girl. You're getting so big I can hardly lift you anymore." She set Grace down and they walked into the front hall where two children's backpacks, one Sesame Street, one Superman, were packed and waiting on the floor.

James rolled Johnny in his stroller outside while Sarah held Grace's hand. Together James and Sarah packed the children into the car and set their backpacks in the back. James waved as Sarah drove the children down the block.

He remembered the first time Sarah saw this house near the ocean, the way her eyes lit up, the way she ran toward it as though she had found a long-lost friend. It was one of the smaller houses in the neighborhood, only a block from the beach, the charcoal gray and white trim exterior a long cry from their wooden home. She loved the house so much, Sarah said, because the triangle windows near the roof were similar to the gables in their Salem home. The proximity to the jagged, rocky coastline was just right, and she swooned as though the house were a storybook villa. The house was a painter's vision of a cottage—white picket fence, stone-lined front walk, wall-to-ceiling windows facing the water, a large garden in front and back yards, and a modern kitchen. James was determined to buy this house for Sarah. He cornered the real estate agent, asked to speak to the owners, and haggled over the price. He was so happy when he was able to tell her the house was theirs.

By the time James returned to the house a storm brewed overhead, the sun disappearing behind darkening clouds. He should work on his book, he knew, yet he couldn't bring himself to go inside. He stood near the door, watching the blue sky disappear behind a kaleidoscope of gray from deep charcoal to near white. Writing a book is such nonsense, he thought. Whoever came up with the idea of torturing yourself to turn ideas into sentences into paragraphs that no one was going to read anyway? But he was an English professor after all, and he reminded himself that he had done little in the way of scholarship recently. The scholarly articles normally came easily enough for him. They were structured and full of jargon and said little enough about anything. But he had written so much about so many subjects over so many years he was wondering once again if perhaps he had finally run out of things to say.

Back inside, James sat at his desk. Instead of writing, he pondered his impending return to Salem. He knew he missed his wooden house in Massachusetts along with the quieter tones of the smaller town. California, as Sarah had warned him before they moved there, was hectic, with too much of everything—too many people, too many noises, too many cars.

He had so many questions then. Should he return to Salem? Or should he stay away? And, most glaring to him in that moment, should he finally leave being a professor behind? As he had said to Sarah, the job had changed over the years. In the not so distant past, being a professor meant passing knowledge from one generation to the next. It meant a meaningful life of the mind where you spent your days teaching the subjects you loved most and your nights researching some papers for publication and some papers for personal knowledge. Now, being a professor meant writing begging letters to fund your research. It meant handling classes of 40 students who expected high grades for putting their names on their papers, who had no problem complaining to the department chair if they thought you gave them too much work, or too little work, or if they thought you were unfair to them for any number of reasons. It meant students with one hundred excuses for not handing their work in on time, or at all. James shook his head at the mere thought of returning to campus for another year. Perhaps his reluctance to complete his scholarly work was telling him something he needed to hear.

Maybe Sarah is right and it's finally time to leave, James thought. But then what would I do with myself? He stared through the open window toward the ocean, still writing nothing. He pushed his laptop away, remembering how he used to write entire treatises with only a quill and prepared ink. Even the ease of technology couldn't make writing easier. What was he trying to write anyway? He didn't know, so he gave up for the day.

He hardly stirred for hours when Sarah came home with the children, her shift at the library done. She walked into James' office and slipped her hands onto his shoulders. Something about the warmth of her hands on his tight muscles always helped him relax. James exhaled. When he turned to look at his wife he saw how she looked more tightly wound than he felt.

"Everything okay at daycare?" James asked.

"Oh, fine," Sarah said. "I don't understand the other mothers, that's all. It's nothing."

"How do you mean?"

"They're so gossipy. Who had a nose job and who had her stomach stapled and who bought a new car and whose husband is having an affair."

"Whose husband is having an affair?" James asked. When Sarah shook her head at him, he smiled. "Sounds like a soap opera."

"Except it's not very entertaining. I feel like such a party pooper when I nod at everyone, listen to them rattle on for a moment, and then leave with some excuse. I'm sure they talk about me as soon as my back is turned."

"You should never be surprised that people talk about you the same way they talk about everyone else. But who cares what they think? They're nothing to us."

"You're right. I can handle feeling uncomfortable for a few minutes. And then I can leave the mean-spirited gossip behind."

"It's like Olivia says," James said. "People who gossip have small lives and they try to make themselves feel bigger by trying to make others look smaller. After, all if Olivia said it, it must be true."

Sarah smiled. "What am I always trying to tell you?"

CHAPTER 7

I consider myself a man of thought and consideration. I am not a man prone to threats or violence. But this night my mind dissolves into a leaking vat of boiled pudding and I scream at the serving girl, horrible things. I accuse her as she accuses my family.

She accuses Father first, but he, being good-natured, laughs at her. He sees no sense or reason in her accusations, that he is Satan's accomplice. She points at him and screams that she sees his specter poking her mother in the ribs. She wipes her hands on her grimy apron and pushes back her gray-tinged cap. She smiles through tea-stained teeth. Then she says things, terrible things, about Lizzie. The girl's horrid words cut through me like a knife at my throat. Her mouth opens like an O that resembles the noose that closed around the neck of our Rebecca. I stand, towering over the servant girl, she is only a tiny thing, after all.

"How dare you!" I yell. I hold my face inches from hers, and though she leans back her face is flat like stone. "How dare you make threats toward my wife, my father, or anyone else in my family? What do you know except how to hurt others? What do you know except how to bring pain to those who have done nothing? What has my father done to you except give you employment, pay you well, and assist your family where he could? What has my wife done to you?"

She smirks in my direction. "Your father thinks he's more important than the rest of us. Just because you come from England. Just because you have money. And your wife. I do not know where to begin about your wife."

Father laughs again. He looks like a spectator at a play, a comedy, the scene all too amusing. "My dear girl, I don't know how I have ever given you that impression. We are all the same in God's eyes."

"God's eyes!" The girl laughs wickedly and points an accusing finger at my father. I shudder when I think of how I saw that finger in the Meeting House pointing out those she and her ilk claimed were possessed by the Devil. "What do you know of God's eyes? You must be tainted by Evil! All Wentworths are tainted by Evil! Twas you I saw sign the Devil's book, wasn't it?"

"All right, girl." The lines round Father's eyes are grooves of indignation. "Tis quite enough. I dismiss you from my home. If you want to accuse me to the magistrates, I welcome you to it. Remember, though, that I am one of the main employers here. If I go to jail, half of Salem Town and a good many in the Village lose their work, as well as their wages, as you now have. You must carry your venom elsewhere."

She freezes as though frustration keeps her bones solid. Then, lit from the inside by vengeance, she pulls her apron off, tearing it in the process, and tosses it into the fire. Burning cotton smells like burning flesh. "Very well then, Mister Wentworth. You reap what you sow."

"I could say the same to you," Father says. Suddenly, the girl is gone, the house silent. Father sits at the long table and leans back in his chair. "Good Heavens! Has everyone gone mad?" He watches the door as if he half-expects her to return in spectral form. "Tis just as well. I have disliked having her in my home for some time now."

"But you have released her from your employment before, Father, and then allowed her to return to her place," I say.

"You are right, Son. In the past I have felt sorry for her because her mother is ill and I know they need her salary. But this is too much. There is no coming back from this. I hope this madness ends soon so everything can return to normal."

As I leave Father's I wonder if anything will be normal again.

Now I am home, relieved to see Lizzie yet afeared at what that young woman will do now that her fury is risen.

After a cup of tea and a plate of biscuits I am settled some. Yet I cannot concentrate on the book in my hand whilst I am distracted by the sight of Lizzie as she putters in the vegetable garden, pulling weeds here, trimming excess there. "You do not need to do that," I say. "Let me hire some help for you."

Lizzie shakes her head and a dark curl falls from under her white cap. "You know I like to feel the dirt on my hands. I am a farmer's daughter, after all." She stands and I smile with the realization that our babe grows within her. I kiss Lizzie and go inside. I am about to pour myself wine to drink when I hear a knock at the door. I open it and see Father's servant girl, who has the nerve to come here after everything she has said. She looks as she did at Father's—bitter, stone-like, shrewd. She appears more emboldened now. She has always been sly, even before the witch hunts, but Father had been amused by her boldness and did not mind her brazenness.

"Well?" she says. I stare at her, unsure what to say. "Well?" she says again.

"Well?" I say.

"Your wife needs assistance. I heard you say so just now."

"You were eavesdropping?"

She shrugs. "I have no work and I must earn. My family cannot live without my wages. I want to work here." She stands on her toes, she is such a puny thing. She flutters her eyelashes and looks at me the way she might look at a lover. "I can help you in many ways whilst your wife is indisposed."

God in Heaven. What have I said to make this girl think I would ever want her in that way? I step back to close the door, needing to get away before I say something to make the situation worse. Yet I cannot help myself. "Girl, you are making a ninnyhammer of yourself. You are mean and low, and there is no woman in the world for me but my wife. Even the blind can see that."

"You don't understand, Mister Wentworth the Younger. People listen to me now. Mister Hathorne and the other magistrates grant me an audience since I see things no one else can. I have power. Even over you."

"Power?" I cough in an unsuccessful attempt to hide my laughter. "Accusing innocent people is power? Tis madness. All of Salem is engulfed in it." I take one step toward her. "Tis not too late to stop. Please. Turn away from your evil doings before tis too late."

"Tis not madness when tis true. The Devil is about in Salem. He sends his scullions to find people to sign his Book."

I scoff. "His Book? And you have seen this Book?"

"I have."

"And what does it say?"

"It says...it says..." She shakes her head. I know she cannot read. "I needn't explain myself. The magistrates know. They understand."

"The magistrates are fools."

"Be careful, Mister Wentworth. They would not like to hear what you say of them."

What is the point of speaking to someone who refuses to hear? This young woman spends most of her life feeling unappreciated and unimportant. She remains unmarried at an age when other women have their own families. She has no establishment of her own and no protector. Now the most prominent men look to her for guidance in ridding Salem of its Unwelcome Visitor. I step back, ready to close the door in her face. "I feel sorry for you," I say. "I do. I hope one day you learn the meaning of the word mercy instead of basking in your own temporary power." I feel a glimpse of sympathy for her, but the harshness behind her eyes snaps me back into horror at what she has become.

"You cannot dismiss me," she says. "I will not allow it."

"Goodbye, Prudence."

She shouts through the closed door. "Perhaps your wife has seen the Black Book? Oh, you will be sorry. All of you will be sorry."

Through the window I watch her disappear into the forest beyond. I try to put her out of my mind, focusing instead on the dinner we are having this night with Lizzie's sullen brother and his contentious wife.

CHAPTER 8

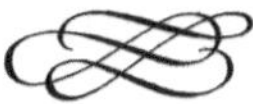

Something changed within James. Sarah was certain of it. She tried so many times to reach him, but he had become withdrawn, even from her. She tried to get him to talk about his days at the university, simple, ordinary conversations they had had hundreds of times, but James shrugged, saying there was absolutely nothing new under the sun to discuss about his job. The university only cared about gathering the students' course fees and keeping them happy so they would stay to pay more course fees, rather than instilling a sense of responsibility for their own learning.

After an uncomfortable silence, James asked, "What do you think they would do, if they knew?"

"What are you talking about?" Sarah asked.

"The children. What do you think they would do if they knew the truth about who I was before? The truth about who you were before. The truth about how our family came back together." He stared at Sarah. He seemed to be challenging her while he waited for her response.

"I think they would love you no matter what. You're their father. They will accept you, all of you. And they'll accept my story too.

They're not old enough now to understand, but in time, when they're older, they will."

When James didn't seem to agree, she leaned her face up as she had so many times. She expected him to kiss her, as he always did, but he stared through her with far-away eyes.

Sarah tried not to be hurt. Whatever was happening with James, she knew it was about him and not her. Still, her heart was stung because during their lives together, their first life and this life, James always lit up gold whenever he saw her, smiling as if he had seen sunlight for the first time in hundreds of years, which he had. Now, there was only stormy darkness behind his sky-like eyes, and Sarah was afraid. Not afraid that he didn't love her anymore. She knew he did. But she worried that whatever it was that disturbed him wouldn't be easily fixed. He wasn't talking, and for the first time, she wondered if their relationship could hold up against her husband's withdrawn nature.

Needing to change the subject, Sarah asked, "Have you been writing in your dream journal like you said you would?"

"You mean my nightmare journal? Yes."

Sarah waited. When nothing more was forthcoming, she asked, "Can I see it? You don't have to show me, of course. I know how personal it can be. But if you wanted to share it with me, maybe we can figure things out together the way we started remembering the past together. It might help."

She watched James' jaw clench as he considered. Finally, he nodded. He went to the dresser by their bed and pulled out his journal.

Why do shadows follow me? Day or night, I cannot escape them. Always the shadows.

Father drives me to the Farms. He had warned against it, knowing my plan, but he knows me well enough to see I shan't be turned from my mission. I have but one task now and I must see it through, no matter the cost to me. What does my life matter whilst my beloved suffers in chains?

Father drives the wagon himself, wanting no eyes to witness us except our own, and Parris'. There are too many whispers about me and, as Father rightly says, I cannot help Lizzie if I am imprisoned as well. Father halts the horse and lets it chew the grass near the parsonage.

Father's sad eyes disappear into his wrinkles. "Are you certain, Son? You know Parris as well as I do. He is not a kind man."

I pick at my skin—my hands, my wrists, my face. I look like the Biblical lepers, but I cannot stop.

"Unclean! Unclean!" I want to cry, but I cannot find my voice.

"James!" Father looks angry, as though he will slap me into sanity, if there be sanity here. "Settle yourself! If you ask Parris to help, then you must present yourself in a manner becoming a gentleman."

"A gentleman?" I laugh, the dull sound dripping with irony. "What use is being a gentleman? Gentlemen and gentlemen's wives are charged with witchcraft every day. No money I offer to pay eases Lizzie's suffering."

"Tis not true, James. We have been able to buy Lizzie bedding. We have secured her proper food and clean water. We have had her removed from..." My dear, kind father cannot bring himself to finish the thought. "Well," he says. "She is no longer there, and that is the point."

I would have vomited but I hadn't eaten.

"Oh, James. Elizabeth is strong. She will survive. And so will you."

I look at the parsonage and sigh. I see no reason to delay. What needs to be done is better now than later.

I say a silent prayer, wondering if my thoughts found their way to Heaven since God and I are not intimately acquainted. How does a loving God watch the happenings in Salem and let it go on? Where is God here? I walk to the front of the house, Father three steps behind, and knock. No one answers.

I press my ear to the door but hear nothing. Father peers through the window and sees eyes peering back at him through open shutters. Suddenly, the door swings open with a thud. I know the woman to be Mrs. Parris. I wonder at her opening her own door until I remember that their slave languishes in prison. According to some, that slave is one of the women who set off this madness in the first place.

Mrs. Parris barricades the door with her sizable frame as if she does not know who to trust. The Parrises have their own share of trouble. Tis hot, the August humidity weighing heavily in the air whilst a low fire burns in the hearth despite the heat. Beads of perspiration line Mrs. Parris' lip. She steps away when she recognizes me and she looks everywhere for her husband. He is nowhere to be seen. She doesn't allow Father and me inside. She shows none of the hospitality we have grown to expect since Father is a respected businessman in the Bay Colony.

The circles of Hell have nothing on Salem.

Then I recall. This is the home of Betty Parris, Reverend Parris' daughter, and Abigail Williams, Parris' niece. Father, sensing my growing fury, squeezes my shoulder.

Suddenly, he is here, Parris. He squints at me and glances round, from Father to me, yet apparently seeing only Father. Parris' hands are clasped before him as if in prayer.

"Good day, Reverend Parris," Father says.

Parris condescends a nod in Father's general direction. Reverend Parris is a scowling, determined man, powerful in his beliefs and firm in his actions. Yet something in him has altered. His anger toward the Villagers has become thin-lipped worry. I would be worried as well if my daughter and niece, children both, wreaked such havoc amongst the innocent.

"Knaves and cheaters," I say aloud despite myself. Father's grip on me tightens.

"What did you say?" Parris squints at Father as if Father had spoken.

Father smiles in an attempt to lighten the mood. But I will not be stopped.

"That is what you have called the Villagers, Reverend Parris," I say. "Knaves and cheaters. Of course, you speak the truth."

"The truth." Parris smirks. He steps toward me, lifting his chin to see into my face. "And what, Young Mister Wentworth, do you know about Truth?"

I look at Father, suddenly unsure of myself. My goal, the only one that matters, slips away from me.

Parris' strong features are etched into a permanent mask of cantankerous impatience, his brow pressing down and his chin pressing up as though his face means to disappear.

"I hope your daughter and niece are better," Father says. "I have not seen

them at the trials. Perhaps these days they are not accosted by vengeful spirits?"

Parris' hair flutters as he turns toward the low-burning fire in the hearth beyond his shoulder. "Christ hath placed His church in this world, as in a sea, and suffereth many storms and tempests to threaten its shipwreck whilst in the meantime He Himself seems to be fast asleep."

The words are familiar to me. They are the words Parris said to Lizzie when she visited them after learning that Betty and Abigail were ill. Lizzie's call was only months ago, yet it seems a millennia. I believe he repeated the lines in a sermon but I cannot recall precisely.

"How may I help you, Mister Wentworth?" Again, Parris addresses only Father. I may as well not be there. And then I realize that I should not have come. I should have left the task to Father, as he said.

Father, seeing how I am tongue-tied, asks for me. "We're hoping, my son and I, that perhaps there is something you can do for Elizabeth, my daughter-in-law. She has been caught up in the accusations. She has been arrested. She is..." Father considers his words. "She is expectant and we fear the babe won't survive, and tis an innocent babe."

I never loved Father more than in that moment. He made the one point that might make this imbecile reconsider his position on Lizzie—the fact that the babe she carries is innocent of any wrongdoing. Of course, Lizzie herself is innocent, but these pompous fools are less concerned about the innocence of grown women.

"Her trial has been postponed until after she has given birth, as is customary for women in her position," Parris says.

"The babe may not survive until then, or Elizabeth," I say.

"James." Father speaks so softly I hardly hear him.

Parris stares through the window toward the farms in the distance. Deep summer sunlight shines like prisms, leaving spots of amethyst and jade on the woven rug beneath his feet.

"There is nothing I can do," he says. He sounds as lost as I feel. "Tis all slipped away from me. I know not why. You can try speaking to Hathorne, but I can tell you now he will not change his mind. He will not relent. He sees the trials as righteous. He believes we must rescue the good people of Salem

from Satan, and of course he is correct. We must save ourselves from Evil. He will not..."

"The good people of Salem!" No cajoling from Father quells the fire within me. "My wife is a good person of Salem! She is good, and kind, and God-fearing. She helps the poor. She helped you! How quickly you forget how she brought you firewood when you had none, when your own parishioners ignored your pleas for more! She worried for your ill children and she helped you! How dare you turn your back on her! You cannot possibly believe she has been touched by witchcraft!"

The puckered expression returns to Parris' face. "I know nothing of the kind," he responds. "Perhaps she is the one who pressured Satan into harming my daughter and niece even more than they had already been harmed. Perhaps she came to spread more black magic over their little hearts."

"Really, Reverend Parris." Father's hearty voice soothes my wretched soul. "I know you do not believe that every person accused of witchcraft is guilty. Even you must know that many innocent people have been accused yet they suffer all the same."

Parris looks defeated. "What I believe is neither here nor there. She has been accused, and she will remain in prison until her trial, which will be held after she gives birth. If she is found guilty..."

Father stepped toward Parris. "My daughter-in-law is ill, Reverend. Now, today, as she languishes in prison, she is ill. As my son said, we are afeared she may not live to see that trial."

Parris sighed. "As I said, you must see Hathorne, though I warn you again, he will not help."

Father and I turn into blinding sunlight. Parris slams the door behind us, shutting out my last hope for rescuing Lizzie. Father leads me toward the wagon. Before I know it, we are back in Town, before Hathorne's house, but tis no use. His maid will not let us see him. She will bring him no message. She knows how to respond to those like Father and me, there to beg for our loved ones' lives. She has turned many away from Hathorne's door. The law is the law, her Master says, and if our accused is innocent of witchcraft it will be revealed at the trial.

Righteous anger burns inside me. My fury knows no bounds. I will see my revenge. And I will make them pay.

. . .

SARAH LOOKED AT HER HUSBAND. Something had snapped shut behind his eyes, keeping her out, over there, somewhere far away. Sarah reached toward James once more, and again he didn't reach back.

"This is just what we expected," Sarah said. "It's about your time during the witch hunts. I remember Hathorne and Parris."

James turned away, and Sarah didn't know what to do for him.

CHAPTER 9

The next day Sarah sent James to the grocery store, asking for some pink Himalayan salt when he knew perfectly well that he had seen some in the pantry. The truth was, he was in no mood for a party. Nightmares, waking dreams, menacing shadows—it was all getting the better of him. Still, he didn't want to upset Sarah any more than he already had, so he put on a smile and went through with the charade. Grace kept her hand over her mouth the whole morning, unable to look at her father without bursting into giggles. Even baby Johnny seemed to be grinning at his father. Olivia kept sneaking outside to text or answer her phone while casting furtive glances, making certain that she was alone.

James pulled Sarah into the kitchen, his arm around her waist. "I already know Geoffrey is coming. Are we having a party?"

"Why would you think that?"

"Because everyone is acting strange and today happens to be my birthday."

"I know. You're 32 today."

"Not really."

"Yes, really. That's what it says on your driver's license."

"Then it must be true."

"Are you leaving for the store now?"

James made a face at Grace, who laughed. "Daddy has to go to the store to get salt because he's 32 today."

When he returned from the market he noticed it was unusually dark and quiet inside the house though he was certain they were home. Sarah knew how much he hated surprises, but Sarah loved fussing over him so he would brace himself and deal with whatever she and Olivia had planned. He opened the door, flipped the light switch, and suddenly people he loved—Sarah, Olivia, Olivia's daughter Jennifer, and James' friend Howard—jumped out from behind the kitchen wall and cheered.

"Surprise!" Grace yelled. "Surprise, Daddy! Happy birthday!" Everyone started singing the birthday song, and James had to laugh, his distaste for surprises left on the other side of the door. Grace sang louder than anyone.

Sarah kissed James' cheek and put her arms around his waist. "Happy birthday, James," she said.

Olivia, her gold hoop earrings swinging in her tip-toe dance movements, her long peasant skirt swaying behind her, stopped soft-shoeing long enough to hug James and kiss his cheek.

"I got you a present," Sarah said. "But maybe we should wait until Grandpa Geoffrey gets here."

"Grandpa Geoffrey." James shook his head. "I can never quite say those words without gagging."

"Be nice to him, James," Sarah said.

Grace said "Gampa!" so loudly everyone laughed.

Sarah shook her head at James. "Daddy is looking forward to seeing Grandpa Geoffrey. Aren't you, James?"

James nodded dutifully. "Yes, Gracie," he said to his daughter, "I'm looking forward to seeing Grandpa Geoffrey."

Jennifer Mankiller, one of James' oldest friends, made her way forward. She hugged him as if it had been decades since they last saw each other. "Happy birthday, James. It's good to see you. You promised you and Sarah and the kids were coming to Oklahoma to visit."

"Is Chandresh here?" James asked.

"He'll be here tonight. With Grandpa Geoffrey." Something about the way she said Grandpa Geoffrey made James laugh.

Howard Wolfe shook James' hand. "Don't forget Timothy. He'll be here tonight as well."

"How could I ever forget Timothy?" James said.

James put his arm around Olivia's shoulders. "So young Mr. Bryston-Wolfe hasn't convinced you to return him, has he?"

"It's not for lack of trying," Howard said. "But he hasn't given up."

"He may as well," Olivia said. "It's not going to happen. I'm never doing that again. It nearly killed me the first time."

James kissed Sarah's forehead. "Thank you," he said. "But out of curiosity, why didn't you wait until tonight to start the party?"

"Grace was so excited that I wanted her to have some fun. By the time the others can join us she'll be ready for bed."

There was a buffet dinner with tapas-style small plates from a local restaurant. Small servings of egg rolls, lettuce wraps, and mini tacos lined the table while an ice cream cake (Sarah's favorite, which James didn't mind having) melted on a platter.

James looked through the window, saw the blanketing darkness outside, and sighed. He knew what was coming, or, more importantly, who was coming, so he settled himself, though he could already feel the muscles in his neck bunching into knots. He helped Sarah put the children down for the night, and he watched the door, waiting.

It bothered James that he couldn't see or hear at a distance any longer. He wanted some warning before Geoffrey arrived. Then there was a banging at the front door and he knew his night was really beginning.

Olivia smiled. "Grandpa Geoffrey is here."

James opened the door, even if he didn't want to. Geoffrey walked in, always looking the same, of course, with silver streaks in his red-brown hair, his large eyes, the same as James', always observant, and his languid way of moving.

"Well! I see you've started the party without me. Not thinking about your very own grandfather. That's appreciation for you." Geoffrey noticed the pile of neatly wrapped presents on the dining room table. "Oh dear! I didn't bring you a pressie. Are you mad, dear grandson of mine?"

"I'm not mad, Geoffrey," James said.

James had grown more used to Geoffrey since moving to California, when they saw James' grandfather occasionally instead of nightly as they had in Massachusetts. True to his word, Geoffrey visited them often since their move across the country, and Geoffrey finally seemed at peace with the fact that James had chosen to be human again. They had so much history, James and Geoffrey, and though James was softening toward his grandfather, there were always those moments when Geoffrey grated on his nerves.

When Geoffrey seemed to be waiting for a response, James said, "I don't need a present, Geoffrey. Just your sparkling personality."

"That I have in abundance. Now." Geoffrey glanced around the room. "What have you been up to, James? You must tell Grandfather everything. Have you been eating properly? Sleeping like a human baby?" Geoffrey squinted at James, up and down, as though determining the truth for himself. "Have you had bowel movements? I hear those are very important for humans."

James was about to say something rude, but Grace had woken up and wandered out of her room. She called "Gampa!" with great enthusiasm, and James carried his daughter into the party. When they were in the living room, Geoffrey patted Grace's head. "Hello, my dearest little great-granddaughter Gracie. How are we today?" He made a funny face and Grace laughed.

"You're still a laugh a minute," James said.

"Yes, yes I am. It's about time you admitted it too. I'm funnier than you are." Geoffrey looked at Sarah. "You know I'm funny, right, Sarah?"

Sarah took Geoffrey's hand. "I do know you're funny, Geoffrey."

"Very good. At least you married a woman with taste."

Soon Chandresh Mankiller, Jennifer's husband, and Timothy Bryston-Wolfe, Howard's son, made their after-dark appearance and the birthday party was complete. James was given the honor of popping open the bottle of champagne and he poured glasses for everyone except Geoffrey, Chandresh, and Timothy, who brought their own beverage, which James realized he couldn't look at any longer, let alone taste. Everyone talked about what they had been doing since they were last together. He overheard Jennifer say, "Now that I'm a mother, I appreciate my mother that much more."

Chandresh, her husband, laughed. "Now that is one thing I never thought I'd hear you say, Jen."

Olivia hugged her daughter. "I always knew you'd come around."

While the others were talking, Sarah cornered Timothy. "How is your gardening business?" she asked.

"It's a landscaping business," Timothy said, "but it's doing well. Turns out you were right. There are a lot of people out there who appreciate having a landscaper who can come at night." He marveled at Grace and patted the top of her head. "I can't believe Grace is so big already. Time moves so quickly for humans."

"That it does," said Howard.

It was a happy affair, and James had to remind himself that this was his life now. He had family and friends and he was surrounded by people who loved him and he loved them in return. After so many years alone, he knew better than to take anything for granted. He knew what happens when you don't appreciate the ones you love, and for that moment, happy in the presence of those who meant the most to him, the nightmares and the distorted shadows were gone. James ate his tapas, blew out his candles, and ate one large piece of chocolate ice cream cake. It was, he thought, the best birthday ever.

DEEP INTO THE NIGHT, their guests gone, James helped Sarah clear away whatever Olivia hadn't already cleaned, which wasn't much. Olivia had been tired out by the party, as well as by her daughter's admission that maybe she, Olivia, wasn't quite as much of a bossy mother as Jennifer had always made her out to be. Olivia slipped into the guest room saying, "Will wonders never cease!"

There were a few dishes left in the sink, so while James washed them he thought of the evening with a smile. Even Geoffrey hadn't annoyed him. Progress, indeed. James stacked the plates and set them in the cupboard. He turned to see Grace still awake standing near the bookcase. Sarah shrugged.

"She couldn't sleep," Sarah said. "Too much excitement today, I guess."

"Too much ice cream," James said.

Grace stared at the photograph she held in her hands. For that moment, James resented the fact that human lives move so quickly. It seemed like yesterday when he and Sarah found the Grace they had been missing at the children's home in Salem. He walked to them and looked at the photograph over Grace's head.

"That's Salem," Sarah said.

Grace pulled the photograph closer to her face as though trying to see every detail. She handed the photo to Sarah.

James wasn't sure how he felt about the picture of their seventeenth-century house. He knew the long wooden slats that made up the exterior walls, the green door, and the gables so well. So much good had happened in that house. But so much bad, and the bad was too terrible for words. These days, the bad was haunting him nearly to madness. He didn't know what to say to Grace, who was looking expectantly at him.

"What are you thinking?" Sarah asked.

"I'm not sure I'm thinking anything." He paused, looking at his daughter. She was too young to understand.

"We're going back to Salem soon," Sarah said. "I think that's a good thing."

"That's what you and Olivia keep telling me."

James knew Sarah was right. He had no reason to hide Salem away as though it was something to be afraid of. Yes, there was a time when the Massachusetts Bay Colony was the most horrific place James knew. Now those days were only memories.

Except when they haunted him.

"It's not good to hide things away, James. Things tend to fester when they're left in the dark."

James looked again at the photograph and knelt next to Grace.

"All right then. Grace, this is our house in Salem." He picked up a second photograph that had dropped to the floor. "There in the background you can see the bay. Salem is near the Atlantic Ocean, and these are the boats in the harbor near where Grandma Olivia has her shop on Pickering Wharf. We took you there all the time when you were even smaller than you are now."

Grace nodded sagely at this new information. How much she understood, James wasn't sure. He took Grace to her bedroom and read her a story. She fell asleep before he finished, and he stroked his daughter's gold curls from her closed eyes and he kissed the top of her baby-soft hair. Before he left the room he kissed the sleeping Johnny's forehead.

One day there would be a reckoning. One day he would have to tell his daughter, and his son, the truth about who he was, who their mother was, who Grace was. He smiled to think that Johnny was the only one of the Wentworths to have a normal human beginning. But James had a story to tell. Sarah and Grace had their stories too. One day the children would have to know, but not yet, not for a very long time, at least.

He recalled his class from the previous night when his inquisitive student struck again with her questions about the witch hunts. This time, she asked about the accuracy of Arthur Miller's play The Crucible. And he told her.

"There is creative license, certainly," James had said. "Remember, Miller was writing The Crucible as an allegory about the madness of McCarthyism. The premise of the story is correct, about the madness of the accusers and how innocent people were arrested and hanged, but the specifics were changed."

"Can you give me an example?" the student asked.

"In real life there was no relationship between John Proctor and Abigail Williams. Proctor was an older, oft-married man, about 60 at the time. There was no proof that there was any witchcraft going on, that is, other than the folk healing remedies that were accepted by most people then. In the seventeenth century, when medical knowledge was virtually nil, people would try anything to cure the many illnesses they were plagued with."

He had to stop himself. He could have gone on, but he said more than enough and the young woman's curiosity was satisfied. Until the following week, at least.

Yes, James thought. There will certainly be a reckoning one day, as much as he didn't want that day to come. He didn't want anyone to know his story; that is, anyone who didn't already know. He especially didn't want his own children to know. After all, he was as human as anyone else now. He had nothing to fear, at least not about that. He joined Sarah, who was sitting on the sofa.

She watched him thoughtfully. Finally, she said, "Do you ever wonder what your life would have been like if we hadn't reconnected in Salem?"

"Never. It's too horrible to even think about."

Where would he be if he hadn't found his Sarah again? He shook his head to make the frightening thought go away.

CHAPTER 10

James could not escape the nightmares.

On yet another night he woke up with a start, his heart racing, his breath bursting in sudden gasps. When he opened his eyes he was certain he had been running from some horror. This one he couldn't quite put his finger on; he couldn't quite touch the vision his unconscious mind had conjured. Dreaming is better when you're dead, he thought. Dreaming when you're alive is terrifying. All of the visions appear distorted as the shapes twisted and turned.

This dream was different. Like his previous nightmares, this wasn't an unconscious message making itself known. This, too, was a memory from then. A memory that James wanted, no, needed to forget. He waited for the remembrance to straighten itself out and appear in a form that made sense. But nothing. For some reason, this nightmare would not make itself known to his waking self. He shuddered when he saw the shadows on the floor. He didn't settle until he realized that the creeping fingers were echoes of the branches from the tree outside the window.

Sarah stirred, and James sat up as quietly as he could. When she settled, he pulled himself out of bed and sat in the wing chair near the window. He wanted to shake her awake and tell her everything. He wanted her to know. He knew Sarah was fed up with his mood swings. But he didn't know what to say, so it was easier to say nothing at all.

He could try to tell her some version of the truth. Sarah, he could say, I'm having more trouble adjusting to being human than I've let on. Sometimes I can't fall asleep at night because for more than three centuries night was when I lived. Other nights I can't fall asleep because I'm afraid of the visions I'll see. Not figments of my imagination. It's like you guessed when you read my dream journal. They are memories from the past. I can't shake the image of you as you were then. I can't make my mind stop obsessing over how you suffered. I see you as Elizabeth, in your seventeenth-century clothing, with your skirts and apron, your white cap covering your cascading curls.

A waking vision of Elizabeth appeared. She was pale, translucent, sitting on a bench in Salem Common with a quilt around her shoulders. She held something close to her chest. It was cold, so very cold, freezing in fact, with ice flurries falling everywhere, leaving the grass slick with ice. The sky was flat gray flannel and the world was frostbitten. She rocked and sang a lullaby, one James remembered his mother singing to him.

If you should die, dilly dilly, as it may hap,
You shall be buried, dilly dilly, under the tap
Who told you so, dilly dilly, pray tell me why?
That you might drink, dilly dilly, when you are dry.

James moved toward his wife, and closer still. He stood over her and saw that she wasn't simply pale but wore a grayish death pallor. She was dead, as was the wee babe she held. James gasped when he realized that the baby was Grace. The Pilgrim-looking people passed without noticing. Without caring. They left this dead mother and her dead baby alone on the bench while the mother's lullaby lingered listlessly in the air. The goodmen and goodwives carried on with their day, untouched by the misery in their midst.

James' ire raged. He felt fury for those who left his Lizzie and child to die in that putrid dungeon. Fury for Parris for allowing the madness to flourish. Fury for those who ostracized him for daring to try to free his wife. Fury for Hathorne, Corwin, and the others who pushed the madness forward. Look what we have done, they could say. We have stopped Satan here. James felt, as strongly as he felt his love for Sarah, that he would never be able to shake his venomous contempt for those responsible. And he didn't know how he would face Sarah with this knowing.

IT WAS ONLY a few days since Olivia had returned to Salem, but Sarah wasn't surprised when she saw Olivia's name on her phone. She pressed the button and held the phone to her ear.

"Hello, dear. I was getting worried. Is everything all right?"

"I think you know it isn't."

"Oh, Sarah."

It was silent on the other end, too silent, Sarah thought. She felt herself freeze, afraid of what Olivia had to say, and Olivia would mince no words.

Finally, Olivia said, "Have you and James booked your flight to Salem?"

"Not yet. I think he's stalling."

"What is he saying?"

"Nothing, Olivia. He says nothing. He locks himself in his study for hours. He comes out to put the children to bed, and then he locks himself back in until he's sure I've gone to sleep. I wake up in the morning and I can see his side of the bed hasn't been slept in. He's usually gone by the time I wake up. I can't get him to open up." Sarah couldn't hide her frustration and she was yelling, not at Olivia, but at James. "You'd think that after everything we've been through, after everything we had to go through to find each other again, you'd think he'd be able to tell me what's wrong!"

"Sarah, you have to remember that James was on his own for a long time. Yes, he had my family throughout the generations, but he was isolated from the world, or at least I'm sure that's how it felt at the time. If someone found out..."

"Yes, yes, I know all that. But I'm here now. We're together now."

"It's hard to give up that kind of solitude overnight."

"We've been back together for three years."

"Three years is nothing compared to three centuries. Besides, you and James haven't exactly had an easy ride of it. First Kenneth Hempel, then the vampire roundups, then Camp Dracula, and suddenly one day he was human again. It wasn't until you moved to California that things settled down, and that's what, only a year?"

Silence again. Sarah felt fidgety, still afraid of what Olivia might say. And then Sarah realized.

"You know, don't you," Sarah said. "You know what's wrong with James."

"Well, yes, dear, I do."

"Olivia!"

"I'm sorry, Sarah, but it's not my secret to tell. James needs to tell you himself."

"James isn't telling me anything himself. He's perfectly content to hide away from me. Forever, it seems."

"Give him time, Sarah."

"Time for what?"

It was Sarah's turn to be silent. She had to think. She knew she had to be honest with Olivia since Olivia would know if she was lying. That's what happens when one of your dearest friends is also one of the most powerful witches, no matter how much she denied it.

"I said this to James when I was in California," Olivia said, "and now I'm saying it to you. You've had an easier time coming to terms with the past."

"That's ancient past, Olivia."

"Not for James. You need to help him deal with the seventeenth century the way you've dealt with the seventeenth century."

"It wasn't one of your magic spells. After the past-life regression, after I remembered that I was Elizabeth, I thought about my life then with James, remembered all of the beautiful things in our life together, and even though the pain was overpowering at times, somehow, somewhere, I knew that dying was simply a change of form. I even knew that James and I would be together again one day. I didn't think we'd be together again literally, the way we are. It was more that our souls would be forever intertwined, so good-bye wasn't really good-bye."

"You've learned your lessons well, Sarah. But James is still caught in the seventeenth century. It haunts him when he's awake, and it haunts him in his sleep. He never changed form the way you did. I mean, he did, but hasn't had a break from 1692 until now. We can pretend that he's 32 all we want, but we both know how old he is. For whatever reason, he's unable to face the stronghold the past still has over him."

"And he's still struggling with being human again. I don't think he cares for human food, even though he pretends to like some things. I don't think he likes being awake during the day, even though he pretends to love mornings and he goes running just to prove his point. He thinks I don't see, but I know him so well."

"You're wrong, dear. James has an inkling that you know. That's why he's hiding away. He has a feeling that you know he's been pretending."

"If that's true then why won't he talk to me?" Sarah sighed. "You're the wise one, Olivia. Isn't it time he moved forward?"

"Yes, but he's going to need help. Which is why you need to set a date to come to Salem."

"He won't ever get to Salem if he keeps hiding from me." Sarah pulled the phone from her ear. She thought she heard Johnny crying, but it was the squall of a seagull sounding through the open window. "I've been thinking maybe I'll take the children and visit my mother."

"In Idaho?" Sarah heard the surprise in Olivia's voice. "Sarah, you and Annabelle..."

"I know my mother and I can be like oil and water, and we haven't always seen eye to eye, but she hasn't been here since Johnny was born and she would probably like to see her grandchildren. And Idaho might bring some peace. She lives in a quiet corner, after all."

"Oh, Sarah. That's such a drastic step. I know things are difficult, but do you want to be away from James?"

"I don't know what else to do. Grace is old enough to sense that something is wrong. She's always asking for Daddy, and I have to tell her he's busy with work when she knows he's in his study on the other side of the door and she's wondering why he won't come out. Johnny is a baby, but I'm sure he can sense something too. Maybe if James and I took a break, maybe if we had some time away..." Sarah began sobbing. "I don't know what else to do. I can't stay in this house while James ignores me. It's too painful. The spring term at the university is almost over. Maybe if I go to Idaho he'll feel more comfortable spending time in Salem with you. Unless you think being in Salem isn't a good idea for him right now. I mean, if he's still so caught up in Old Salem..."

Olivia sighed. "Please don't go to Idaho, Sarah. Not now. James needs you now."

"But..."

"Give me a few days, dear. Let me think. Between the two of us we can figure out what to do for the best. You and James are *beshert*. It's destiny that the two of you are together again. It simply isn't possible that your marriage is meant to end this way. Hang in there a few more days, please, I beg you. There's a way through this where you and James come through the other side even stronger than you started, I know there is."

Sarah agreed. She hung up the phone, dried her eyes, and stood in the doorway to the children's room watching them sleep. He was such a miracle child, Johnny, when Sarah considered everything that had to happen to bring him into the world. And she would never forget their darling Grace they had been missing. That child she carried all those years ago was there with them, as if by magic. They had so much to be thankful for. If only James could see that.

But Sarah would do as Olivia asked. She would wait. For now.

CHAPTER 11

Sarah sat on the edge of the bed, her suitcase open, the inside empty. What do you pack for a trip you're not sure you want to go on? She watched her husband. For the first time since their marriage, she thought she saw a stranger. James was already packed, but he glanced around, pulling out drawers, searching the closets as if he had forgotten something.

"Do the children have everything they need?" James asked.

"I've checked their bags three times. They're fine." Sarah wanted to reach out to her husband. All those years, whenever she needed comfort he was the one she looked to. But now there was a wall between them she didn't understand. She tried to will James to look at her, at least in her direction. Instead, he walked to the window, unlatched the lock, and pressed the glass aside, allowing the ocean breeze to tousle his hair. Though his back was to her, Sarah saw his pained reflection in the glass.

"The salt water reminds me of Salem," he said. There was such sadness in his eyes. She wanted to go to him, kiss him, pull his arms around her, but Sarah didn't know how to break across the divide between them. "Are you sure we should do this?" he asked. "Go to Salem, I mean."

Sarah shook her head. "It's either go to Salem or…"

"Or what?" James took a long step toward Sarah and frightened her with his suddenness. "Or what, Sarah?"

"Or I go to Idaho with the children."

"What do you mean go to Idaho? You haven't said anything about us going to Idaho."

"Not us, James. Me. And the children. I was making arrangements to take Grace and Johnny to Nampa to see my mother. She hasn't seen them since Johnny was born."

"You don't even like your mother, Sarah."

"It's not that I don't like her. We just, well, we're different people and we don't always see eye to eye. But she is my mother and our children's grandmother. And I need to get away."

James looked as though he had been slapped by an invisible hand. "Get away from what?"

Sarah exhaled. It was time. She had to say it now or it might never be said.

"I have to get away from you, James. I don't know what has happened to you. I don't know why you're so cold and distant to me of all people. You are my dear and loving husband and you can barely bring yourself to look at me. If you're…" Sarah had to stop. Her throat was closing and she couldn't breathe, but she pressed on. "If you're tired of me, of our marriage, of any of this, I decided I would give you a chance to think about it, about whether or not you want to be married to me. Because I can't live like this. I can't live with you like we're roommates sharing a house. I love you too much. I have loved you for too long and I can't…" She dropped her head into her hands as she struggled for the right words. "I need some space, James, and more importantly, I think you need some space from me. I think we both need time to consider where we're going from here."

James dropped with a thud into the wing chair near the window. He looked as though he didn't understand what Sarah said. He was stunned into silence. The coastal wind blew through the room, leaving Sarah chilled in a way that felt like she would never be warm again. She watched her husband, waiting for some reaction, anything that would let her know that he had heard her, that he knew how deeply she was hurt by his aloofness. He looked out the window and sighed.

"You would seriously consider leaving me, Sarah? You don't want to be here?"

"How can I be here when you don't seem to want to be with me anymore? Is there another woman, James? Are you in love with someone else and want to leave me?"

James stood up. He looked angry now. "Are you asking me that question? Do you think I could ever love anyone else?" His voice was loud, his words cracking under the weight of his emotions. "I spent 300 years miserable and heartbroken. I wrote you letters. I thought of you every moment. In more than three centuries I have never loved another woman, not ever, and now you think I'm in love with someone else? It's like you don't even know me."

"You're right, James. I don't know you. Not the way you've been acting lately. You're a stranger to me, and I never would have thought that was possible, not between us."

James paced the length of the room, one end to the other, again and again, watching his feet as he moved. Then he sat on the bed beside Sarah, taking her hand. He leaned his head close to hers and looked into her eyes.

"I am not in love with any other woman. I couldn't ever love another woman." He closed his eyes, and when he opened them again Sarah saw the deep hurt. In an instant she understood that it wasn't another woman keeping James cold and distant.

James kissed Sarah's hand. "Olivia said that you and I need to go to Salem. I agree with her, especially if the other option is for you to take the children to Idaho without me. I can't risk losing you, not again, and not like this."

"So there is something you're keeping from me."

"Yes, but it's not another woman."

"You don't like being human again, do you?"

"You know?"

Sarah couldn't stop smiling. "Olivia said that you guessed that I knew."

"Well, I had an inkling that you might. You rival Olivia with your ability to understand what isn't said."

"You're right, of course. I did know. Or at least I guessed. But I need to hear you say it."

"All right, yes. I've been having trouble getting used to being human again. I thought that since I wanted it so much it would be easy. I thought that since I was human before it would be nothing to return. But I've been struggling. I still haven't developed a taste for human food. I like the sunlight at times, but at other times it's simply too bright. I love the cover of night. To me, darkness is a soothing blanket that keeps the world out and only us in. Most nights I have trouble sleeping when it's dark."

Sarah put her hand to her husband's cheek. "Why couldn't you tell me that?"

"Because there's more to it. You already know about my nightmares about Old Salem. I can't shake the anger, Sarah. I don't know how you've moved past it because I can't. Whenever I think of how they treated you, what they did, how you died." James' voice cracked, and Sarah's heart swelled with sorrow.

"Oh, James. You need to let it go."

"I can't. I get so angry I want to murder."

"They're already dead, you know." James shrugged, a sad smile on his lips. "That's why Olivia told us that we need to go to Salem. Salem is where it happened, and Salem is where you need to put it to rest. Olivia said that we need to work this out now, James, or our marriage may be gone forever. The bond we've had will evaporate. That can't be part of the plan, not now. We have to solve this together, you and I. I refuse to give up on our marriage, and I refuse to give up on you. You can get past this, James, and if anyone can help you it's Olivia."

"I will never give up on us, Sarah. I love you too much."

Finally, they were both reconciled to the fact that they were returning to Salem. James brought the tailless black cat to the pet sitter's that night and they left for the airport before dawn.

CHAPTER 12

James and Sarah weaved their way through the crowd in Logan Airport, Sarah wheeling Johnny in his stroller, James carrying a sleeping Grace. They saw their favorite witch waving at them through the glass door.

"Sarah! James!"

Olivia clapped her hands in front of her face as if she hadn't seen them in years, though it was only a week since James' birthday. She lowered her voice and kissed the sleeping Grace in James' arms. Then she kissed the top of Johnny's dark hair while he stirred, yawned, and leaned back in his stroller.

"How were they on the flight?" Olivia asked Sarah as they made their way through the parking lot.

"Surprisingly good. Grace listened to James read her about two hundred stories and Johnny sat on my lap the entire time."

"Did you try the towel soaked in brandy?" Olivia nodded sagely. "Works every time."

"No," Sarah said, laughing. "We didn't want to get arrested for getting our baby son drunk on an airplane."

Olivia waved her hand, knocking the thought away. "Everyone does it, Sarah. But you're lucky. You have two beautiful angels here."

Olivia smiled again at the children. She looked from Sarah to James, and Sarah knew what Olivia was thinking. But things had become less tense since James opened up about his struggles with being human again.

Olivia clicked her black key and the lights of the silver Prius flickered. "Here we are. Everyone ready to go home?"

Olivia noticed that James was visibly nervous now that they were getting ready for the last stage of their journey. Yes, Olivia thought. He needs to be here now. He must work through whatever ails him here. Miriam agrees with me. And Miriam would know.

James lifted the hatch of Olivia's car and set his family's luggage in the trunk.

Olivia pointed at the back seat. "I even remembered the baby seat for Johnny."

Olivia exhaled as she drove toward home. No matter where she was in the world, and she traveled often, she always longed for Salem. James was right. She would never leave. As she relaxed and grew more comfortable, James grew more tense. He sat straighter, his face harder, as though steeling himself for some horror he could not name. James closed his eyes and held his breath until Olivia nearly asked him if he needed to go to the hospital. Finally, he exhaled and Olivia sighed with relief. It was still a shock for her to remember that James breathed again. Thanks to me, she thought. Only she wasn't sure that what she had done was for the best.

OLIVIA TURNED down the road near the bay and Grace pointed when she saw Olivia's white cottage. It was April, the height of spring beauty, and Olivia's rose garden was in full bloom while sweet floral scents filled the air. James opened the car door for Sarah, then helped her to unstrap Johnny from his safety seat and Grace from her seatbelt. He carried Grace and Sarah carried Johnny past the trellis-lined walkway to Olivia's front door. The coastal breeze brushed James' hair from his eyes, and Sarah smiled. She remembered the man she found in Salem four years before, the man whose gold hair constantly fell into his face. She remembered the first time she saw him outside their house, how he had frightened her since she didn't realize anyone was home. In quick-time motion, events fell into place and she could hardly keep up. Once they knew who they were to each other, once she remembered their past, everything was all right. As long as they had each other, they would always be all right. It had to continue that way, Sarah thought. She couldn't bear the thought of what might happen if it didn't.

Grace woke up and cried when she found herself in a strange place. She saw Olivia and smiled. "Gamma!" she called, and Olivia was only too happy to take the little girl into her arms.

"Oh, my dearest Gracie. How are you? You've grown so much in the past week! Are you happy to see Grandma Olivia?"

Olivia walked Grace around the house. "Do you remember Grandma Olivia's place, dear? It's been so long since you've been here. You were quite a little girl then."

Grace, who wanted to walk herself, kept saying, "Put me down, Gamma!" until Olivia let the little girl run around the house with her gold curls flying behind her. Grace examined everything—the cozy country-style furniture, the photographs in antique frames, the vases of roses set out on white doilies. The gray tortie cat asleep on the back of the sofa received special attention.

Olivia smiled at Sarah. "I can never decide who she looks more like, Sarah, you or James."

James carried the sleeping Johnny and set him down in the middle of the bed in Olivia's dayroom. "I hope that's all right," James said. "I wasn't sure where you wanted everyone."

"That's perfectly fine, dear. You can help me lug the crib down from the attic. There hasn't been a baby sleeping in this house since Jennifer was born."

James began unpacking Johnny's bag. When he was no longer in hearing distance, Olivia leaned close to Sarah and whispered, "I can sense what you're thinking."

Sarah shook her head. "You know how much I don't like that about you, Olivia."

"Believe me, being able to sense thoughts is no gift. I've spent most of my life trying to block out the noise."

"I thought you couldn't read thoughts."

"You're right. I can't read them exactly, but I can still sense what others are thinking."

"And James?"

Olivia shook her head. "Oh, James. He blocks me out like he has a cement wall around his mind. With James it's more of an educated guess."

"He's the same with me. What is it you always say? This too shall pass."

"It will, Sarah."

Sarah watched her husband closely. Something about his expression made her think that he knew how important this time in Salem may prove to be.

CHAPTER 13

No matter how many times he left and came back again, James always marveled at how Salem looked the same. Even with the newer restaurants, the tourists shops of psychics and tarot card readers, the modern businesses and homes, there was a sameness that James appreciated. Over the years, whenever he missed Salem, he thought of the soft ripples of the bay, the water undulating in ebbs and flows. Even when he lived near other coastlines, he missed the whispering Massachusetts shore. It was strange for James to realize that he had hardly seen daylight here. Of course, he saw the sun when he first arrived with his father in 1690, he saw it briefly when he met Kenneth Hempel at the library, and he saw it again after Olivia returned him. For James, Salem meant darkness and night, a life shrouded in shadows with only the moon and the stars. He avoided people as much as he could, afraid they would see into his too-dark eyes and know that he was not what he pretended to be. He avoided eye contact and he avoided making friends, a solitary soul whose life consisted of teaching, researching, writing, and dreaming about his wife.

Now he looked at Salem in the daylight and he couldn't believe how different everything appeared. It was a warm April and there had been an early start to the tourist season. Sightseers made themselves obvious in their khaki shorts, Salem Witch t-shirts, and walking shoes, their cell phone cameras at the ready. He was now a visitor himself, noticing his surroundings as though seeing them for the first time.

James and Sarah had a wonderful time taking Grace and Johnny around town. They took the children to Salem Common, a tree-filled grassy park. They ate their picnic near the white gazebo, and when they finished they walked down Washington Square. Later that day, James borrowed Olivia's Prius and they visited Salem State University. Sarah and James brought the children into the library, a brightly lit, multi-story facility with the latest computers and more study desks than before.

"They've improved it so much," Sarah said.

"It worked perfectly fine for me," James said. "I met a lovely librarian here. The most beautiful woman I've ever seen."

"Who was it?" Grace asked.

James put his arm around Sarah. "It was Mommy, Grace. I met Mommy here. Meeting Mommy was the best thing that could have happened to me." He tickled Grace until she giggled. "Now you and Johnny are also the best things that could have happened to me."

"Actually," Sarah said, "if you remember correctly, we met for the first time outside our house."

"Outside our house?" Grace asked.

"That's right," said Sarah. "I went to look at the house because I thought it looked like someplace I knew, but then suddenly your father was standing there and I thought I knew him too."

"I knew your mother the moment I laid eyes on her," James said.

"How could you know her if you didn't know her?" Grace asked.

It was such an innocent question, yet it was impossible to answer in a way that made sense to a young child so James and Sarah let the subject drop. They walked across campus, resting for a moment under one of the plentiful trees that lined the walkways. They arrived at Pickering Wharf and strolled along the boardwalk, passing the Witches' Lair, closed since it was Olivia's day off. They bought pretzels and lemonades and window shopped at the antique and fashion boutiques.

"There's the Friendship," James said, pointing to the three-masted ship. "Let's go see it."

They walked to Derby Wharf and stood before the replica of the tall ship the Friendship of Salem The ship had been built to replicate the original vessel from the late eighteenth century.

"This ship was built to symbolize the maritime trade and how that trade helped the United States grow in the early years," James said. "The original vessel carried cargo like silk, coffee, candles, tin, sugar, salt, and cheese."

"It sounds like what your father used to trade in," Sarah said.

"You remember that?"

"Vaguely, but yes."

"Father traded in rum also."

Sarah stepped close to the ship, the masts snapping in the rising wind. "You know, in the three years I lived in Salem, I don't think I ever actually visited this," she said.

"Me either," said James. "I think because it reminds me of the days when Father spent hours at the dock negotiating or supervising the ships he had built here. The original Friendship was built around 1797, which is about a century after Father had his ships, but the style of the vessels hadn't changed much in that time. If Father could see this, he would find it quite familiar, I think."

"Your father worked with pirates," Sarah said.

"Yes, some of them were pirates. Father spent days, sometimes weeks, negotiating prices for the goods he traded. He built our house where he did because it was in easy distance of the wharf."

"Where's our house?" Grace asked.

"We can go see it," Sarah said.

They walked alongside the bay. They passed the House of the Seven Gables, where there was a crowd gathered to visit the house made famous by Hawthorne's haunted tale. Then, down the street, they turned right and saw their house.

Sarah had to restrain her tears when she saw it. The wooden

gabled house was being leased by the Salem Historical Society, and there were tourists taking pictures and admiring the seventeenth-century garden. But it was no museum, not really. To Sarah, it was her home. James put his arm around Sarah's waist and pulled her close. She wiped her tears away with the back of her hand. "I'm sorry," she said. "I'm surprised at how much emotion I feel seeing it again. I know it's only been a year, but it feels like so much longer."

"I know the feeling," James said. "I've lost track of how many times I've left and come back, and every time I see it again I feel the way you do now."

The last of the sightseers dwindled away. It was after five o'clock, the tours were over, and James smiled when he pulled the key to the front door from his pocket. "I made sure they didn't change the lock so we could get in if we wanted to."

Sarah grew weepy again when they were inside. The house had been restored to its seventeenth-century glory, with the furnishings and kitchen restored so visitors could see what a seventeenth-century house looked like. To Sarah, it was like no time had passed. It was 1692, and she was home with her beloved James. There was the cauldron in the hearth, the copper pans hanging on the kitchen wall. There were wooden stairs leading up to the loft where they kept their trunks filled with heavy clothing and extra blankets for winter.

Grace was mesmerized. She ran her hand along the wooden slats that made up the walls and she sat in one of the seventeenth-century oak side chairs. In the kitchen, she tried to touch a copper pan hanging on the wall just out of reach.

"Do you want to see it?" Sarah asked. She handed Grace the pan and Grace turned it over in her hands.

The next morning, their dear friend Martha appeared at Olivia's front door. Martha swept the children into her arms as though they were hers to keep forever. Martha was still Martha, heavy set, smiling, her jet black hair still cut into a flapper's bob. She asked James and Sarah about their life in California, and she agreed to visit them on the West Coast. Martha joined the Wentworths on their trip to the Witches Lair where they were meeting Olivia.

The spicy scent of sandalwood incense invited them into the shop. Olivia appeared from behind a bookcase with open arms and she greeted everyone with a hug and a kiss.

"Martha!" Olivia said. "What a lovely surprise. I'm so glad you could join James and Sarah today."

"Wow!" Grace's eyes were wide, and she seemed amazed by the gothic ambiance of the Witches Lair. She pointed at everything around her as though everything she saw was indeed magic.

Olivia flipped off the overhead lights and turned on the electric sconces high on the walls, leaving the shop in mystical darkness. The Witches Lair still had shelves overbrimming with books of spells, crystal balls, packets of incense, and tarot cards, and toward the back were small rooms for psychic readings set off from the rest of the store by black velvet curtains. An antique cash register sat at the front of the shop on top of a glass counter with baskets of silver rings, amulets, and crystals.

Sarah pointed at the cash register. "You know we do that with our phones these days. We can pay and everything."

"Pooh." Olivia shook her head. "The world is becoming too dependent on electronic doo-dahs. If you want to see real magic I'll show you real magic. Keeping that old cash register in working order is a feat of the highest order."

Sarah laughed. "You sound like Geoffrey."

"Geoffrey does know what he's talking about," Olivia said.

"Sometimes," James said. "Maybe."

It was a beautiful day, the sky clear except for an occasional cloud passing overhead. In the distance, a boat motor hummed while tourists lined up at the coffee bar. Customers wandered into the Witches Lair, and Olivia answered their questions and completed their purchases. One young woman bought a book of love potions, which she clutched to her heart as she hurried away. Olivia shook her head.

"Poor girl. There's nothing in that book that will make the man she loves look her way."

Another customer came in to examine the crystals. Olivia rang up her purchase of several amethysts. After the shoppers cleared away, Olivia nodded toward the partitioned-off rooms. "Remember the first time you were here, Sarah? That reading I gave you?"

"Of course I remember. You nearly scared me out of my wits, though I didn't want you to know it at the time."

"Why not?"

"Because I didn't want you to think I was weak or easily scared. I didn't want you to know how much your words affected me, especially since I didn't know you very well at the time. I certainly didn't understand what you were trying to tell me."

"You didn't want me to think you were weak or easily scared? That's so human, isn't it?" Olivia glanced at the clock on the wall and saw that it was noon. " I thought we'd have lunch at Cap'ns. But first there's someone in the back who wants to say hello."

Olivia led everyone to the dark storage room. She lit three taper candles sitting high on a shelf, and then a dark-haired young-looking man appeared from behind a tall stack of boxes, his white complexion bright as though lit from within.

"Timothy!" Sarah held her arms out. "I'm so happy to see you again so soon."

"I'm happy to see you too," Timothy said. He gave James a big hug, which James was happy to return. Timothy had a hug for Grace and he patted Johnny's head. He leaned toward James and squinted. "Are you going to say goodbye to the witch trials now that you're here? That's what Olivia said."

James shook his head at Olivia. "You didn't expect me to keep a secret from Timothy did you?" Olivia asked. "We're leaving for lunch, Timothy. Will you be all right sleeping back here?"

"I'll be fine. Don't worry about me." Timothy hugged James again. "I'll see you again before you leave, okay?"

"You're acting like we haven't seen each other in years," James said.

"I know," said Timothy. "But twice in one year isn't enough."

James clasped his former student's shoulder. "I agree."

James and Timothy shook hands, and Olivia steered the humans toward the door. They walked down the wharf to Cap'ns where they sat outside under an umbrella that fascinated Grace. After ordering iced teas and fish and chips, they watched the high-tide bay leapfrog toward the ocean. It was a quiet afternoon with only an older couple eating at a nearby table. Martha nodded toward the water.

"You know, the witch hunts were really about women," Martha said.

"Do we have to talk about the witch hunts?" James asked.

"Yes," Olivia said. "We do."

"It's always better to talk about things openly than leaving them to fester in the gloom," Martha said. "I don't mean just the witch hunts here, but throughout New England and in Europe as well. The hunts were about fear of the power women hold. Did you know that in the ancient past humans used to worship goddesses? The goddess was the holiest of the holy, and her power to bring forth life was revered. When religion became patriarchal, everything was about subverting women, controlling them, keeping them in their place. Whenever women were seen as outside of that place they had to be made an example of, and that's what happened during the witch trials."

"But men were involved too," Sarah said. "What about Giles Corey? What about John Proctor? What about James?"

"It started with women," Martha said, her southern accent a beautiful singsong. "First they blamed women, then they made scapegoats of them. Families had no problems turning in their wives, mothers, daughters. You mentioned Giles Corey. He got himself involved in the accusations by suggesting that his wife had bewitched him and others. It wasn't until he realized that they were taking him seriously that he retracted his accusations. When they asked him to name names he refused and his punishment from the court was to be crushed to death with stones. Everyone lived in terror of being accused and arrested." She looked pointedly at Sarah. "Your own family offered you up as a witch. Where do you turn then?"

"It was the madness," James said. "I've always said it was the madness."

James couldn't hide the frustration from his voice. The pain. The sorrow. James had that faraway look in his eyes that Sarah knew all too well. Sarah leaned away from her husband, and for the first time since they arrived in Salem, Olivia was afraid for James and Sarah. She couldn't let this problem between them grow. She knew it was up to her to intercede on their behalf, to put the two halves of James and Sarah together again.

With one glance, Olivia knew that Martha understood everything.

"People go mad when they feel as if the world is out of control," Martha said. "Isn't that right, James?"

James nodded but said nothing.

Olivia returned to the Witches Lair, and James, Sarah, and the children walked Martha to her house, which wasn't far from Pickering Wharf. After kissing their friend, James took his family back to Olivia's, where he faced one more restless night of shadows and madness.

CHAPTER 14

That evening, Olivia unlatched her backyard gate and paced to the bay, staring as the sun's rays faded like lavender pools into a violet horizon. Soothing wisps of fading waves comforted her, as they always did. She stopped at the edge of the shore while cool foam covered her toes, her Birkenstock sandals on the sand behind her. She lifted her gypsy-style skirt to her knees, and the only sound besides the breeze was the jangle of her hoop earrings. Salem at dusk had always been her saving grace. No matter how difficult her day had been, no matter what problems she dealt with, magical or otherwise, she had always been able to steady her mind in that scenic spot at land's end. Most problems are a result of thought, she knew. Over the years, Olivia had learned that real problems occurred often during our lifetimes, but our reactions to those problems were determined by us alone.

What others saw as an unflappable serenity about Olivia, Olivia knew was simply knowledge passed down the generations. From her family she learned that ultimately we already had the answers we needed if we were brave enough to look. What seemed like a simple, even boring life to others brought satisfaction to Olivia. She didn't need much to be happy. She loved her little shop where she sold mysticism and spells. She loved the outdoor patio where she, along with her closest friends, held Wiccan gatherings, casting spells of healing, hope, and love. She loved giving palm or tarot readings to customers, most of whom began as skeptics, though usually she won them over in the end. Sometimes, a customer from a year before would make a point of stopping by to tell her that what she had predicted had come true. The person had received the raise, or moved across the country, or fell in love, or got divorced.

Olivia was pleased when people came to tell her their stories. There was something comforting in Olivia's manner that made her someone people wanted to confide in. She could never bring herself to tell them the truth, that she couldn't remember anything from the palm or the tarot readings. She went into a trance when she was in touch with the spirit realm, and when the trance ended she had no recollection of anything that had happened during that time. Fortunately, only a few people complained about her messages, so Olivia didn't mind too much that she had no memory of what she said. She didn't need to know what occurred since it wasn't about her; the messages from beyond were not intended for her. She was only the messenger.

Occasionally, people were angry at what Olivia said. She had given them bad news. The person they loved didn't love them back. They weren't right for the job they were training for. The marriage, which they were determined to save, was hopeless. Olivia tried to tell them that change, even change that seems negative at the time, is often a precursor to the greatest good.

"You have to let go of the things that aren't working to make space for what belongs in your life," Olivia told them. Sometimes, her words appeased them. Sometimes, they fell on ears that refused to hear. Olivia would refund their money and let them go. She could not control their reactions, only her own.

People are so resistant to change, Olivia thought, yet change is the only promise in life. She remembered sitting with her mother near the fireplace in their little cottage only miles from where Olivia now lived. Life is about change, Ayelet, Olivia's mother, would say.

"We are always changing form, Little One," Ayelet said. "We change form when we leave the spiritual realm to inhabit our human bodies. Change occurs throughout our human lives as events shape us. And then we change form again when our souls pass on." Ayelet, like Olivia, always had her eye on the horizon, drawn to the bay like the life-giving force it was. "It's sad how humans cling to this life as if it's all there is." Ayelet winked at Olivia, who was nine at the time and becoming privy to her mother's magical secrets. "There is more to the universe than our senses tell us, Livvie. You must always remember that."

A seagull passed overhead, flying so low it nearly landed on Olivia's head. Her close-cropped hair was more silver than red now, and Olivia welcomed the visible signs of progressing through life. It has been a good life, Olivia thought. She said a prayer of gratitude, then smiled at the seagull, nodding as though they shared a secret. The bird squawked and glided near the water.

Always, Olivia welcomed change, even when it was painful. There were joys too, and she knew that focusing on those joys made this life beautiful. Olivia smiled when she remembered yet again the first time she met Sarah. Jennifer had invited Sarah to attend the Wiccan ceremony they were holding at the Witches Lair. Sarah came into the shop, her dark eyes wide as she scanned the bookshelves. In one glance, Olivia knew that Sarah was searching. For what, Olivia didn't yet know.

Even before Olivia noticed Sarah's searching, she noticed Sarah's sadness. She looked weighted down, Sarah, as though invisible hands pressed her toward the ground. It took some cajoling, but eventually Sarah agreed to a palm reading in one of the private rooms. Olivia's gift came most alive when she touched someone hand to hand. Sometimes, there was a sharp jolt, a flash of electricity. Sometimes it was a feeling, inchoate, and when Olivia fell into a trance she couldn't remember it anyway so it didn't matter.

Although Olivia couldn't remember what she said to Sarah that day, she knew that she had been in touch with spirits, enough to awaken Sarah to the supernatural world. That knowledge opened

Sarah's heart to James, to their truth, to the secrets they shared. To their love. Sarah knew James, even changed as he was in those days, and she loved him as he had always loved her. They were *beshert*. There was no getting around that. Olivia smiled at the waves as they slid toward the shore, the moon flashing its silver face directly above. Ah, Salem. There were so many places Olivia loved, but she could only live in Salem.

She remembered why she had been thinking of Sarah, and her smile faded into small-lipped fear. James and Sarah. Whatever was she going to do about James and Sarah?

She was at a loss as she had never been before. James and Sarah's love was destiny. They were meant to be together. How could this estrangement between them happen? How could they possibly have problems in their marriage?

"It isn't possible," Olivia said aloud. The seagull, gliding again, squawked in response. Olivia looked at the bird. "Yes, you're right. It isn't possible that they should pull away from each other. But James is so stubborn. Oh, I could strangle him, he's so pigheaded sometimes." Olivia waited, hoping for some response from the bird spiraling in graceful circles. When the bird remained silent, Olivia shook an agitated finger upward. "Being like that, are you? Fine."

Olivia paced along the shore. She dropped her skirt and after two short waves she was soaked to her ankles, but she hardly noticed. She was focused on James and Sarah.

"I don't know what to do." Again, Olivia waited, and again, the bird was silent. "Is it up to me to save their marriage? James has to learn to communicate with Sarah. He thinks he's protecting her but he's only causing her worry. Doesn't he realize that Sarah is serious about taking the children to Idaho? Yes, she's here with him, but then he closed down again at lunch. Of course Sarah noticed. But what can I do?"

Olivia felt lightheaded, the way she felt when the spirits called her. She focused on her breathing and listened.

"Is anybody there?" Her voice was a whisper in rhythm with the waves. She asked again, "Is anybody there?"

The wind swirled with tornado-like speed and the seagull was swept away. The waves rose like noontide and the crashing water slapped the shore. Olivia held her hands near her ears. Then she raised her arms to the heavens. This Prospera needed no fairy-friend to make the seas do her bidding. She raised a tempest before her, the nor'easter whipping the coastline every which way. Looking every bit the sorceress she was, she felt electric as her wet skirt slapped her legs and her silvery hair stood on end, her earrings singing like wind chimes.

She lifted her chin toward the dark sky and nodded. "Yes," she said. "I hear you." She tipped her ear to the heavens, her closed eyes taut in concentration.

The words were so clear. Anyone could have heard them.

"Salem is where it began," a woman's voice boomed. "And Salem is where it shall end. Here where you stand is the beginning and the end of their story. Wherever they go, Salem will be there. Unless they acknowledge the truth."

"You mean he," Olivia said. "Unless James acknowledges the truth."

"He!" the voice boomed. "He must say it. He must face it. All of it. Or their story will come to an end. Forever."

Olivia lowered her arms. The seas calmed, the storm cleared, and the peaceful night resumed. Her breath settled and she opened her eyes, finding the Salem shore exactly as it had been, the sea receding as the hours treaded toward dawn, the moon sinking. The seagull reappeared long after seagulls should be seen, spiraling once more. The bird squawked, and Olivia nodded.

"Yes, I heard," Olivia said. "And now I know what to do."

CHAPTER 15

Clanging metal grates my brain like cheese, as though someone drags one of the links along my spine. I would jump out of my own skin if I could. I stand at the bottom of the staircase, squinting into the shadows until my eyes adjust to the dimness. There is no natural light since the prisoners are underground and there are no windows here. The stench makes me ill.

After a jarring moment of blackness I notice a dim stream of sunlight showing through cracks in the locked, heavy door that keeps the prisoners inside the dungeon. Then I see the pitiful beings chained to the walls. I visited this horror one week ago, yet all has changed. The women look weaker, thinner, wisps of their former selves, barely alive. I squint into the void, searching the faces. Some of the women sit, some press themselves against the wall as they attempt to stand, their legs quivering beneath them. Others lie down on the dirt ground. I do not see Lizzie.

"Lizzie?" I call. I am more frightened as the moments pass. "Lizzie, tis me, my love. Tis James. Where are you?"

Chains rattle, and I hear a cough, light at first, but the hacking becomes more severe.

"James." Lizzie's hoarse voice rises from my right. "I'm here."

I follow the sound to my beloved. I cannot stop myself from shedding tears at what I see. In a week, Lizzie has grown so weak. She looks skeletal, her beautiful eyes sunken, her lips cracked. I reach for her.

I want to tell Lizzie something wonderful. I want to tell her that everything is all right now, I will rescue her. Father has found the help we need, and she will leave this Hell very soon.

And then I realize that to say such things would be a lie, and I have never lied to Lizzie. I may not always tell her everything, but I do not tell my wife bold untruths. I cannot tell her that her case is past hope. I cannot have her lose whatever faith she may have left. Does she have any remaining faith at all while languishing in a putrid dungeon for a crime she hasn't committed?

And then I do what was unthinkable only a moment before.

"Tis all right, my love. We have found help from the highest of places. You will not believe who is on our side. Father believes we can have you released before long."

Even in that dim light I know that Lizzie knows I lied. She smiles sadly. She shakes her head but says nothing.

I take Lizzie's hands between my own. Her hands are so frail, so thin, I am afraid if I hold them with too much pressure they will splinter into dust. I outline the bones of her wrist with my fingers.

"I need you to stay strong this little while longer, Lizzie. I need you to be brave."

"I am brave, my James," Elizabeth says. "I have trust in God, and you. I know that things will work out the way they are supposed to. Sometimes we do not understand why things happen the way they do. But know this. You will always be my dear and loving husband. No matter where I am, no matter where I go, you will always have my full heart. I want you to move on, James. I want you to have a happy life. For my sake."

"Lizzie, what are you saying? You are my heart. You are my very reason for breathing. Who am I without you? There can never be anyone else. Who else understands me the way you do? No." I step away. "This sounds too much like you are saying goodbye and I forbid it. You will survive this, you will give birth to our child, you will be proven innocent of witchcraft, and we will return to England as a family. Do you understand me?"

A single tear sears Lizzie's cheek, and I raise her chin so I can see into her eyes, black pools in the dim light.

"I will never say goodbye to you, James," Elizabeth says. "I will always be with you. I will always be here."

The prison guard grabs my arm. "Time is up. You must leave."

I press my lips to Lizzie's. I cannot help but think she is already cold.

I begin, "If ever two were one then surely we."

"If ever..."

The guard drags me away and shoves me through the doorway, locking Lizzie into the dungeon on the other side. I stand before the door, my hand on my lips, still feeling Lizzie's touch.

If I do not rescue her this day it will be too late. Fortunately, I believe Father has a plan.

CHAPTER 16

James awoke shivering, cold rivulets trickling everywhere along his skin. The blanket did nothing to warm him. Sarah was already gone with the children to visit Olivia at the Witches Lair, where she had been spending most of her time since returning to Salem.

James pulled himself out of bed, draping his still-shivering frame with his bathrobe, wondering when the nightmares would end, if ever. He wandered to Olivia's rose garden, an enchanted place of secret lawn chairs behind shady birch trees and hummingbirds poking their delicate beaks into flowers. Wind chimes sang in the sea breeze and roses of every shade bobbed on their trellises in greeting. Olivia's garden had always brought James peace, particularly when the buds were in bloom. He tried to still his breathing, and for a moment he considered the meditation that Olivia insisted was good for him, but he shook the thought away as silly. He studied the tallest tree, hoping to find some answers and discovering none.

Still feeling anxious, James wandered back inside, meandering through Olivia's empty house, standing near the French windows that looked into the front garden overflowing with wisteria, lavender, and violets.

Olivia's voice echoed in his head. "Don't focus on the negative, dear. You need to let the past go."

James thought about his nightmare of remembrance of that despicable dungeon. Elizabeth, like other prisoners, had been tortured. She had been blocked between two walls pressed tight against her sides, frozen in an agony of tearing muscles and popping bones. She couldn't sit, she couldn't stand, their unborn child suffering in silence. He hadn't seen her between the walls himself, but she told him. He knew, and he felt as though he had been tortured too.

James had that antsy feeling that overwhelmed him whenever he was consumed by worry. His own skin weighed him down and he had an urge to claw his way out of it. He opened the back door and returned to the rose garden, sitting once more on the lawn chair beneath the tallest tree. He breathed freely for a moment until the rush of emotions overwhelmed him again. He hunched over, his hands on his knees, panting, a position he found himself in many times in those days. How do humans deal with this pain day in and day out, for decades, even a century? After a year of wearing mortal coil, he still hadn't a clue.

He wandered toward the seashore. It was a quiet midmorning, the sun breaking through the overcast clouds. There had been a storm during the night and the humidity lingered and the air was heavy. In the distance, James saw Pickering Wharf. He went back inside the house, dressed, then headed in that direction.

He wanted desperately to see Sarah. He wanted to pull her into his arms and kiss her lips and rest her head against his chest. He still didn't know what he wanted to say to her, so he turned and walked the other way until he stood on the beach again. He felt as if he were going in circles, which he was. He sat on the sand where the bay swept the shore. He took his shoes off and rolled his trouser legs up and stepped into the cold water, which sent goosebumps along his skin. The beach was deserted, unusual for a warm spring day. No tourists lingered, or locals, only a mother and two small children swimming near the sand. James watched them, shielding his eyes with his hand.

Suddenly, he heard a voice echoing in his head, a familiar voice, a hearty stage actor's voice with good humor underlying the loving heart. "She is here, James. She is well. Your children are well. Be happy."

James shook his head. "Oh, Father." His words fell easily into the rhythm of his native accent. He had been born in London, after all, in 1662. "I cannot. I do not think I can even be here. There is too much sorrow. There is too much damage done. Too much horror. I cannot forgive them."

"Elizabeth forgives them."

"She is called Sarah now. And she has always been a better person than me."

Suddenly, the voice echoed so loudly James couldn't make sense of his father's words. He looked around as though, if he turned his head quickly enough, he could catch a glimpse of his father before he disappeared. One day, James feared, his father may stop visiting.

"Father?" James called. But John was gone. "I need you, Father. I don't know what to do. I don't know what to say to Sarah, but I'm afraid she's going to take the children and go and I can't lose her again. I know I can't. Father?" James waited, hoping for some sign that John had heard him, but nothing. Perhaps James had imagined it and his father was never there.

A severe sadness shook James to his core. He watched the waves roll toward him and recede, again and again, and still he didn't move. He watched the white cotton clouds float past with one last hope that he might see his father, but when there was nothing but the sky he shook his head, exhaled, and walked past Salem Common, which was crowded with sightseers and locals alike. Salem was such a tourist hotspot, with its museums and historical landmarks denoting the places important to the Salem Witch Trials. Every year tourists rode the red trolleys around town listening to tour guides explain how Salem is likely short for Jerusalem, which means City of Peace. James watched a family of tourists snap photographs of the statue of Roger Conant staring across the town with a sneer, as Conant likely did in 1626 when he arrived in the Massachusetts Bay Colony searching for a better life. James shook his head at Conant, guessing the Pilgrim-looking man would have been a magistrate in the witch trials if he had been in Salem then. James crossed the road and stood before the Salem Witch Museum. More tourists entered the church-like building, and James realized he had never been inside. He didn't need to go in. He knew the events better than any docent, any historian. He had watched the tragedy play out before his eyes.

He meandered through town, this way and that. He knew his way around blindfolded, and the way he walked, his eyes closed, his fists by his sides, he may as well have been blindfolded. Finally, he saw it—his own wooden gabled home. He had seen it only the other day, but for some reason the sight of it impacted him more strongly during this second viewing. He stood across the street, watching sightseers take pictures of the wooden sign banged into the ground, "Wentworth House," it said. Costumed docents led groups around the property, showing them around the historically accurate gardens in front and back, through the great room, pointing out the hearth where Lizzie cooked their meals. There was a small cafe to the side that served clam chowder and lobster rolls, and visitors sat with their meals at picnic tables. James jangled the keys to the house in his trouser pocket. Who were these strangers poking through everything, peering in the corners, sitting at their dining room table, standing over their bed? He reminded himself that it was his idea to loan the house to the Salem Historical Society. They might as well earn an income from the house while they were in California, he had convinced Sarah. It seemed so logical at the time, but now, watching his house overtaken by people who didn't understand the truth of their story, he regretted the decision.

He followed one group beginning its tour; in effect, he looked at his own home through the eyes of a stranger. The docent, a young university-aged woman wearing a white cap, long skirts, and an apron, explained the historically accurate herbs growing in the front garden. Then she led them inside.

James didn't need to listen. This was his home, after all. Then something the docent said caught his attention.

"One night, in August 1692, at the height of the witch hysteria, the mistress of the house, Elizabeth Wentworth, was accused of witchcraft and arrested. Her husband, James, son of the prominent merchant John Wentworth, pleaded with the local magistrates to free his wife, insisting that there was no proof of any wrongdoing by Elizabeth."

The docent was blank-eyed, as if she had repeated these lines too many times for the words to have any meaning for her. The group she spoke to listened with various degrees of interest. Some waited for her next word with bated breath. Others were more focused on taking photographs. Others, mainly children and teenagers, couldn't have cared less as they watched videos on their phones.

The young docent continued. "Historians believe that Elizabeth's husband, James, was himself suspected of being a wizard. There was a hunt for him when he disappeared suddenly around the time of Elizabeth's death. James Wentworth had become suspected of witchcraft because of his odd behavior after Elizabeth's arrest. Some said the odd behavior came from his devotion to Elizabeth and his fear for the outcome of her trial. Elizabeth's trial was postponed until after she gave birth since she was pregnant when she was arrested. James petitioned everyone he could find to help his wife. He wrote to Increase Mather, a much-respected Church figure at the time. He pleaded with Samuel Parris. All to no avail. James sat entire days outside the jail waiting for someone who might help him. At times, he appeared to be talking to himself. Some said he spoke through magical means to his wife on the other side of the prison wall. Some said he spoke to the devil, making a pact that would free his wife. Some said he had lost his mind in his grief and spoke to himself. Many times his father, John, would come in the middle of the night to lead James away. And then one day he was gone, never to be seen again."

James felt nothing as he heard his life story related to a pack of strangers. A list of facts to be memorized and recited. That's all his life was to them.

Cold, James thought. I feel so cold. I haven't felt this cold since I was... He dropped his head into his hands. Dead, James thought. This is what it feels like for a human to be dead. My grief means nothing here.

He had never given any thought to what the people of Salem had thought of him then. He only cared about Lizzie. According to this docent, they attributed his disappearance to witchcraft. They weren't far off, he thought bitterly. It was black magic of another kind that changed him beyond recognition. Black magic he still didn't understand and probably never would.

The tour continued, but James couldn't listen any longer. He needed to get away. Each step became quicker than the one before until he was running.

He stopped out of breath down the road while memories of his last days with Lizzie flashed before him. The vivid vision of Lizzie's accusation, his desperation as he tried to convince her to leave Salem forever. They had already planned to return to England so James could resume his studies at Cambridge. His father had promised him a start in life. But the passage across the sea was dangerous for everyone, most especially for newborns and new mothers, and Lizzie didn't want to take the chance.

He was the head of his little family. It was his decision to make. Why didn't he pack her up and take her away? Damn it, he knew! He knew what was happening in Salem but he didn't want to force her to go on a journey she was afraid of. He had been so certain that, despite the horrors surrounding them, nothing bad would touch them. Every day, others were arrested or executed for witchcraft when they weren't witches, but James couldn't believe the worst would happen to Lizzie. Who would want to hurt Lizzie?

Then, finally, he convinced her to leave. They were leaving the next day, in fact. But fate got in the way.

Fate. Why was it so cruel? James wondered aloud, "Why Lizzie? Why me?" And then he realized. Why not Lizzie? Why not him? No one was exempt from the madness that engulfed Salem. Everyone suffered the same.

When he could breathe freely again, he made his way back to Olivia's.

CHAPTER 17

Olivia watched James as he drank his coffee at her dining room table. He was hurting, and though much had been made clear by her nighttime seance by the shore, there were still things she didn't understand. The spirit world was less than forthcoming that morning and she had exactly zero ideas about how to achieve her plan. She wanted to snap her finger or wiggle her nose and invoke the good feelings spell, but that would be a band-aid on a deep wound that needed cleansing and stitches to heal. That was her job, she decided—to help him heal. From the way James looked at her, she thought he was waiting for her wise words, but at that moment she had none to give.

"Perhaps I need another reading or one of those woo-woo spells you love so much." James grinned at Olivia.

Olivia shook her head. "Magic isn't always the answer, James. Often, the best answers are the ones we discover for ourselves."

"I was afraid you'd say something like that."

"That's it, isn't it?" Olivia clapped her hands, her smile lighting up her features. "I understand what she was saying. It's all so clear now! You need to discover your answers for yourself. I can show you the way, but it's not something I can do for you."

"You don't need to look so gleeful."

"But I should look gleeful since I understand now. I thought I understood before, but I realize I was only at the beginning."

"In English?"

Olivia swatted James' shoulder. "Stop making fun."

"I'm not making fun. I'm trying to figure out what on earth you're talking about."

Olivia stepped close to James. She stood so close their noses nearly touched.

"And now for the hard part," Olivia said.

James leaned away from Olivia. "And here it comes."

"I challenge you, James Wentworth. I challenge you to be brave enough to discover your own answers. If you want to leave the nightmares behind, if you want to repair the rift between you and Sarah, you'll be willing." She eyed James, half-expecting him to protest, but he sat silently, waiting. "You need to discover for yourself why you're unable to put the past behind you."

"But I already know what's troubling me. And so do you. Being human isn't as wonderful as I remembered it to be. I see now how I idealized my human life. I only remembered the good things. I forgot what it was like to be mortal and I made human life out to be something magical and extraordinary."

"Human life is magical and extraordinary, James. But you have to allow yourself to see it that way. If you focus only on the negative then you'll only see the negative. Here, I want to try this exercise with you." Olivia sat beside James in the floral chair near the window.

"Now listen to me. I want you to look around the room and pay attention to everything you see that's brown. Ready?"

"Is this necessary? I…"

"Ready?"

"All right, all right. I'm ready."

James studied the room, making a mental note of all things brown: books, tables, and the hardwood floor.

"Have you seen everything brown?"

"Yes, Olivia. I've seen everything brown."

"Good. Close your eyes. Are they closed?" James nodded. "Now I want you to name something in the room that is green." James opened his mouth to speak, but nothing came out. "Name at least one thing that is green. Can you do it?" He shook his head and Olivia smiled. "You can open your eyes now."

"What was the point of telling me to notice the things that are brown if you were going to ask me to name something green?"

"To prove my point, dear. When you focus on one thing only, you fail to notice anything else. You were so focused on the brown that you neglected the greens, the blues, the yellows, and everything else for that matter. When you think of the past, you are only focused on the negative."

"The negative was horrific, Olivia."

"Yes, it was. But even with the horror, there were still good things. You and Elizabeth created a simple, happy life even in the midst of that madness."

"When I look back all I can see is the faces of the people who accused Lizzie and jailed her and tortured her until she died."

"Then that's what you have to face. You won't be able to see the full palette of color until you stare it down."

"I face it all the time. I can't think of anything else."

"We've been through this before. You think about it every day. But you aren't facing it. You haven't faced the reality of what that time did to you."

"I'm still at a loss about how you can say that to me."

"I repeat, James, you have thought about it to obsession, but you have never faced it. You need to stand toe to toe with those memories, as hard as they are. You need to face them head on and you need to acknowledge the horrendous impact they've had on your life—yours and Sarah's. Your memories are tearing you to shreds. They are dropping man-sized stones on your head, but you're turning away."

"I was writing the dreams down."

"But you stopped."

James threw his hands into the air. "Yes, I shredded the dream journal. So what?"

"You can't shred your truth any longer. It's your turn to face the shadows so they can't control you anymore."

"How did you know about the shadows?"

"I know everything, dear. Don't you know that by now?"

James' expression morphed from anger to fear, his internal struggle passing like lightning across his handsome features. He pressed a stray lock of hair from his closed eyes.

"I don't suppose there's any way out of it," he said.

"No," Olivia said. "There isn't."

James sighed. "All right then. Where do we begin?"

Olivia grabbed her bag and her keys and led James to her car in the driveway, locking the door behind them. They didn't speak as Olivia backed her car into the street and headed for the highway toward Danvers.

At least, it is called Danvers, Massachusetts now. In previous generations it was known as Salem Village, the epicenter of the Salem Witch Trials. Olivia saw the grimace overtaking James' features when he realized their destination and she wondered what was going on in that pretty head of his, though she didn't have to stretch far to guess. They arrived in Danvers and Olivia drove down a quiet road. To the right was a seemingly ordinary farmhouse.

"It looks the same," James said. "The Nurses' place."

"Does it? That's good. You need to see it the way it was then."

"Why?"

"I'm not sure. I just know it's right." They drove in silence until they arrived. "We're here, James."

Olivia got out of the car, but James was stubborn. She opened the passenger door, waiting.

"When was the last time you were here?" she asked. James shook his head. "You don't know or you won't say?" James said nothing. "Take your time, dear. Just take your time."

James steeled himself and got out of the car. He could not stop staring at the house.

"Are you ready?"

"What am I supposed to do?" he asked.

"Whatever you feel you need to do. Walk around, see the house, remember that time."

"I've told you a hundred times that I remember that time every single day."

"Face the memories here, right now, at Rebecca Nurse's home. Stop skirting around the issue. Stop repressing. Think about Rebecca. Think about how much you and Lizzie loved her. And yes, you must think about what happened to her too. By the time we leave here, I want you to make peace with it."

"Make peace with the fact that an innocent elderly woman was hanged for a crime she didn't commit?"

"Yes, James. That's exactly what I want you to do."

"And how on earth am I supposed to do that?"

"By forgiving them. Sarah has forgiven them. Now it's your turn."

James turned away. He said, in a whisper, "Why doesn't anyone think I know my own mind? When I say I can't forgive them, I mean I can't."

"Yes, dear, you can. But first you have to accept what happened. Accept it without judgment. It happened, there was nothing you could do to stop it, and you must acknowledge that."

They both bought a ticket so that they were allowed into the museum. James had to force himself to walk inside the Rebecca Nurse Homestead. Part of him felt as though it were all new, as though he had never seen it before. He felt like any other tourist visiting an interesting spot connected to the witch hunts.

At first, James didn't move. He stood in the middle of the main room staring at his feet until Olivia nudged him.

"I'm here, James," she said. "Don't worry. I'm right here."

James stared at the furnishings in confusion. It was all so familiar, yet not. He realized that he hadn't been inside since 1692. Certainly, he knew the homestead. Sarah—Lizzie—visited often. Lizzie had been close to Rebecca Nurse.

Olivia stood by his side. "It's your turn now, James."

"I still don't understand exactly what you want me to do."

"You will, when it's time."

James hated it when Olivia spoke in riddles. Suddenly, he felt himself pulled back through the centuries. He was not in Rebecca's house, but his. He saw the entirety of his first life play out before his eyes. He saw Lizzie across the table where she spoke gently to her much younger sister. He felt the joy-filled sparks as he fell in love with her. Then he was at their simple wedding where his father insisted upon Indian Pudding. He relived the first time Lizzie saw the beautiful wooden house John had built for them. He stood firm in his connection with Lizzie, how she understood him, and he understood her, how they were content in their quiet life together. He touched the smile on Lizzie's face when she told him they would be parents. And then, always, the ultimate sorrow at the end.

That's where he was stuck, he realized, just as Olivia said. He was stuck in the sorrow.

He was in his own world now. He didn't see the tourists. He forgot about Olivia. In his mind, he and Lizzie were at Rebecca's. It was a journey from Salem Town, where James and Elizabeth lived, to Salem Village. Elizabeth's father, Silas, lived in the Village too, alone after her sister died. Whenever they traveled to see Silas, they made a point to stop and see Rebecca. Lizzie's mother died when she was young, and although Rebecca was closer to Lizzie's grandmother's age, Lizzie looked to Rebecca as a mother figure. James saw himself and Lizzie in the front room of Rebecca's house. Lizzie and Rebecca chatted away while James and the men of Rebecca's family discussed the finer details of land management and farming practices.

James came back to himself as the docent began speaking about how Rebecca Nurse had been caught up in the madness of the witch hunts. The young woman's facts were basically correct, with perhaps some rumors and half-truths thrown in, but her voice betrayed none of the emotion of those caught up in it, just like the docent at his house. He was annoyed at first, but then he realized—how? How could this woman know about having family and friends whisper about your supposed unholy doings? As the docent moved toward the next area of interest, James stayed behind, lost in the memories. The last time he and Lizzie visited Rebecca, the madness had engulfed

Salem, though neither Rebecca nor Lizzie had yet been caught up in it.

Olivia's voice came as a whisper on a breeze behind him. "Think of what Rebecca meant to you and Elizabeth. Remember, James."

So he did. He remembered when Elizabeth first introduced him to the kindly older woman. Rebecca Nurse smiled at James in her grandmotherly way and James was immediately taken in by her friendly manner. If anyone needed help, Rebecca was the first to give it. Rebecca was always to be found at church, her head bowed in fervent prayer. She was a devout believer. And look what it got her, James thought bitterly.

He walked outside and stared at the land surrounding the house. He had stood there so many times with Francis, Rebecca's husband. Francis Nurse was always interested in James' opinion since James helped his father in the mercantile trade. Francis was happy to share ideas with someone with a head for business.

"Tell her," Olivia said. "Tell Rebecca what you've wanted to say to her all these years."

In his mind's eye, James conjured Rebecca Nurse. "I'm sorry, Rebecca," he said aloud. "I'm sorry this happened to you. I'm sorry how people you should have been able to trust treated you so viciously. How could anyone accuse you of witchcraft? Your accusers, even in the moment of their accusations, must have known their lies. Yet people believed them because it was convenient. Perhaps the lies made them feel better about themselves, or perhaps they helped them make sense of the madness. I'm sorry people can be so cruel. I'm sorry you were falsely accused. I'm sorry."

All those years later, he still couldn't face it.

"Say it!" Olivia demanded. "You need to say it out loud, James. Until you acknowledge the horror, all of it, you'll never be able to move on."

James shook his head. He struggled to fill his lungs with the oxygen humans needed, but Olivia wouldn't budge. Finally, he closed his eyes.

"I'm sorry you were hanged, Rebecca," he said. "You were an innocent woman and you were executed, and no one should be made to suffer like that." His head fell to his chest. He felt like he had aged to his true age, which was more than three centuries. "Sarah and I, Elizabeth and I, will always love you." His voice creaked in a whisper. "We'll remember you for the good, kind woman you truly were."

Olivia slipped her hand into James'. "Well done, James. Now let's move on."

As they headed back to Olivia's car, James was afraid to ask where they were going next. He sat silently while Olivia got back onto the highway toward Salem. When Olivia turned down Essex Street, James guessed where she was headed.

"We're not going there, are we?" he asked.

"Maybe."

"Oh, Olivia. That's the last place I want to go right now."

"Which is precisely why you need to go. I don't know how you lived in Salem on and off for so many years and never went."

"I never went because I was afraid of what I'd do if I did. I probably would have gotten myself arrested for destroying public property."

"I'll bail you out of jail if it comes to that, dear."

"Thanks, Olivia."

Olivia parked her car and led James toward the Old Burying Point Cemetery.

CHAPTER 18

James had avoided this place for centuries. Of course, he passed it when it couldn't be helped. Whether driving or walking, whenever he was on Charter Street near the Peabody Essex Museum he stared straight ahead as if he had blinders on. Mainly, he had been successful in his quest to never look upon it again. Olivia wandered to the gate, went inside, and read the ancient-looking headstones, shaking her head as she paused over each name. She saw James lingering, his face blank, his shoulders hunched, his eyes downcast.

"He's been here for hundreds of years," she called to James, "and he'll be here when you're ready."

James paced from one end of the block to the other. His thoughts scrambled and he tried to rearrange them into something resembling coherence. He was still struggling with the very human sense of panting for breath while your heart beat a quick-time tune between your ribs. He grasped the wrought iron gate in an attempt to keep himself upright. The graveyard was empty except for two tourists who wandered the grassy grounds with its twisted trees of skeletal-like branches and a view of the surrounding brick buildings. Olivia continued to read names and dates. She stopped in front of one in particular and caught James' eye, waving him over. James wanted to follow, but his legs wouldn't obey. When he finally stood beside her he saw the grave of Bartholomew Gedney, one of the triumvirate of witch trials magistrates, along with Hathorne and Corwin.

Olivia led James to another stone. Like the Ghost of Christmas Yet To Come, she pointed at the grave before her. James gasped aloud when he saw the name John Hathorne.

"What do you have to say to him, James? What have you waited all these years to tell him?"

James took no time at all to recall the harsh features, the thin lips, the small eyes. Hathorne had been a wealthy merchant like James' father; in fact, John Hathorne and John Wentworth had been friends before the madness. Hathorne played such an important role in condemning "witches" through "trials" that were shams of justice. Even the magistrate's great-great-grandson, the author Nathaniel Hawthorne, who added the w to his name so that he would not be too closely connected to his ancestor, said that Hathorne *made himself so conspicuous in the martyrdom of witches, that their blood may fairly be said to have left a stain on him.* What hurt James the most was the fact that Hathorne never apologized for his part in exacerbating the disaster. Even after people realized that innocents had been executed, Hathorne remained silent, taking his secrets to the grave. Whether he had any guilt about his role in the travesty, no one would ever know.

James had envisioned this scene so many times, but now that he was there his mind was blank. For a moment, he hardly remembered who Hathorne was. Events from the late seventeenth century disappeared from his mind, leaving him oddly empty since the seventeenth century was all he had thought about for months. Until he remembered. Then his face grew hot and his blood boiled like fresh-flowing lava. If he could have done so without getting arrested, he would have dug up the magistrate's grave with his bare hands and strangled the man's bones.

James turned to Olivia. "I need to do this alone."

"Yes, I believe you do." She took two steps toward the open gate. "I'll be right there, dear." She pointed outside the Old Burying Point.

"Take your time." Olivia turned a heavy glance onto James, as if seeing through him to the very marrow of his soul, as was her way. When her stare became invasive, James turned away.

He touched the grave and sighed. The headstone was framed by granite to preserve the original stone. They preserved it so I can spit on it, James thought, or other things he would not name even to himself. He read the headstone aloud: "Here lies the interred body of Hathorne ESQ Aged 76 years Died May 10th 1717."

Hathorne lived 25 years longer than Lizzie, James thought. How very wrong.

He conjured another vision of John Hathorne, that sorry excuse for a man who took his job of removing demonic influences from Salem as seriously as he took himself. Suddenly, James heard Olivia's voice. He turned to see her, but she wasn't there. He was certain he heard her, though there was nothing now but bird songs.

When James was alone in the Old Burying Point, he pointed at the headstone.

"You!" he shouted. "You took nonsense imaginary testimony and treated it like the most important words ever spoken. You were responsible for sending innocent people to their deaths. I can hear you now, making excuses for your abominable behavior, saying that everyone believed in evil spirits then. People believed that Satan existed, pushing people to do sinful things for sinful reasons. Did you believe that? Or were you simply trying to make yourself look good for your pride? Did you need to show everyone how important you were? Were you demanding respect? Did you never consider how your decisions affected others? People died because of you. Real people with real lives who were hanged! My wife died, ill and alone, in prison. Did you feel no remorse? Did you feel nothing? You took my wife and it was hundreds of years before I found her again. It's only because I was..." James kicked at the grass until he felt Olivia prodding him. He was certain he could feel the presence of others, specters, perhaps. "It's only because I was turned that I was able to find her again." James laughed. "You were so sure of yourself, convicting innocent victims accused of evils of all sorts, and meanwhile devils ran free turning people like me into immortal beings. Only you were so blind you never saw the truth. You only saw what you wanted to see."

James burned with the need to kick the preserved stone until it shattered. Then he remembered that he no longer had the strength for such a feat. When he regained control of himself, he found Olivia outside the graveyard watching traffic move past.

"Come, dear," she said. "There's one more place you have to go." James shook his head and set his jaw, determined not to follow her any longer. "You're so close, James, so very close. I can feel it. Don't give up now, I beg you. You must do this if you're ever going to be free."

James knew Olivia was right. He was nearly there if only he could be brave this little while longer. And he would be brave. For his Lizzie.

JAMES WAS TAKEN to one more graveyard he had been avoiding.

Olivia turned the car off and sat for a moment, her motherly features focused on James, trying once again to see through him. He didn't stir, and the silence between them was foreboding. She said nothing. She waited. And waited some more. When he was ready, he unlatched his seat belt and opened the car door. He still didn't leave. One leg was on the pavement, and one leg was inside. One-half of him was ready to face this, the other half wanted to continue burying his head in the sand.

"I'll wait here, dear," Olivia said. "I'll be right here if you need me."

This cemetery was uphill from the shore, a wire fence the only barrier stopping visitors from tumbling into the water. The land stretched to the edge of the water with a bird's eye view of the houses beyond. The day headed toward dusk, the dropping sun turning the clear sky first yellow and then a dusky pink while an iridescent mist blew in from the bay. The stoic houses in the distance watched his every move, and his own wooden gabled house was particularly intrigued. The setting sun glowed across the gothic-looking headstones leaning this way and that, the weight of the ages pushing them askew. The cemetery was deserted except for the man who knew where he had to go. He was only steps away from his final destination on a day of painful truths. But he couldn't bring himself to move. In all those years he had never visited. Like the Old Burying Point, he passed this graveyard so many times. When he was a preternatural man, he could see it through his front windows. But he pretended it wasn't there. Now he didn't think he could handle the agony, especially since his heart was human once again. Human hearts could break, as he knew all too well. His preternatural heartfelt pain was enough for one thousand lifetimes, but his human heart would tear in two under such a heavy burden.

In the space of a breath the graveyard was half in shadow.

Always the shadows.

James had been here exactly once. It was night since he could only live at night then. At the time, he found her grave, wept blood at the sight of it, and he sat there unmoving, statue-like, until dawn broke in a celestial light and he had to make haste to escape before he was struck by the sun. He nearly hadn't left in time. He thought, with the bitter taste of his blood in his mouth, that he would rather stay there until he didn't exist any longer. He would rather be burned alive or suffer from whatever happened to his kind when they were struck by sunlight. Who wants to go on living when his Lizzie was no longer beside him? No longer there to experience life with him, no longer there to share his joys and sorrows? And their child. Oh, God, their child was buried there with Lizzie. The poor lass never had a chance. No, James had decided all those years ago. I would rather die than live without Lizzie. He sat before his wife's grave, his neck and chest wet with his blood, making peace with his impending death until his survival instinct overtook him and he disappeared into the gloom.

Once again, James was compelled by a force he didn't understand. He ran between the ancient headstones until he stopped in front of the one he didn't want to see.

Elizabeth Wentworth. Beloved Wife and Mother. Died 1692.

An animal-like groan bellowed from somewhere deep within.

James screamed, nonsensical words, speaking in tongues, perhaps, while shaking his fist at the sky.

"How could I let you down, Lizzie? I love you so much." He dropped to his knees, heaving under the weight of the anguish he held inside too long. "Father tried to warm me. If only I hadn't been so stubborn and left Salem as soon as the madness started. If only I had listened! How could I be so stupid? My stupidity caused this. And you, oh my God, Lizzie. You died! And I couldn't help you but I promised I'd help you and there was not one thing I could do. And then I had to live all those years alone. How could those people do such terrible things to so many people? Didn't they care how you, how any of you, suffered? And what about those who died at the gallows? How dare they! How dare they make pronouncements about who lived and who died. And you died, Lizzie! Why?"

A puff of wind from the bay brushed James' hair like a sweet, soft breath and he felt calmer. In an echo of a breeze, he heard Olivia's voice. He glanced around but didn't see her.

"But then you wouldn't be here now, James," Olivia said. "You and Elizabeth would have been long gone, and who knows if your souls would have been drawn together again in quite the same way. It was the pain that caused you to reach out to each other again. It was the pain that brought you together again. Who are we to know the universe's plans?"

"You still haven't explained why it's the universe's plan for people to suffer."

"It may not be the plan, but suffering is part of human life on earth. Human beings have free will. We use that will for good, but not as often as we should. Humans are driven by survival instincts, and when people think their survival is at risk they make cruel choices, often involving anger and violence. But there's more to this life than our eyes can see. There is so much we don't understand."

"I've told you this before, Olivia. I still refuse to believe there's meaning in horror and violence."

James stood at the edge of the graveyard, clutching the fence as though he were afraid he would tumble head-first into the water. He stared at the darkening sky while the heavy clouds overhead looked ready to soak Salem with rain.

He heard another voice echoing through his mind. One woman's voice poking and prodding him, pushing him toward...what? He wasn't certain, though he recognized the voice.

"What is wrong with you, boy?" the woman said. "Have you learned nothing? Have you sat with your head in the sand whilst the waves washed your brain so clean you think nothing? How much have you experienced? How much have you seen?"

"That's just it, Miriam," James said. "I have seen and experienced too much. Don't you realize how much wrong there is in the world?"

"You are too caught in the past." She snickered at him, her sarcasm heavy in the brisk sea breeze that snapped at him with shuddering force. "Look forward, James Wentworth. Tis the only way."

"Where is forward?" James asked. "You mean today? Are things so much better now? Are people so much wiser? Does no one shout false accusations from the mountaintop? Is no one belittled, abused, or killed as a result of the false beliefs of others? What is there to be done?"

"We can only do what we can do, boy. If you stand up however you can, whenever you can, then you give others the courage to do the same. And then others, and then others."

James clutched his aching head in his hands. "There's too much madness. It will never leave."

Joining Miriam was the hearty voice that lifted James' heart.

"There is beauty in the world, Son. You know there is. You and Lizzie experienced so much joy in your lives together. You must forgive them."

James sat stubbornly on the ground. "No. I won't."

"You must."

James would have shaken his fist at his father but he couldn't bring himself to do it. He had no energy left. A shadowy figure appeared before James, and he recognized the ghostly outline of his father. John Wentworth, his slight frame, his wise eyes, his face a map of the world, was visible so that the human James could see. James would have laughed at how the scene reminded him of that moment when Scrooge is shown his grave, only this wasn't James' own grave. He would have gladly seen proof of his mortality instead of the grave he now sat before.

"Should I bargain with you?" James asked, his voice cracking. "Should I promise to do better in the future?" The waves of the bay splashed the shore with more strength. John Wentworth's form remained still, unmoving.

James punched his fists into the rocky ground, into the hard gravestone itself, into his legs, bruising himself though he didn't feel it. He let out every sadness, every anger, every loneliness, every frustration he ever felt for over more than three hundred years. When he was spent, he traced the name Elizabeth Wentworth on the headstone.

"I don't know how to make this right, Lizzie. I'm sorry."

Footsteps crunched on the dry grass. James looked up, expecting to see Olivia, but it was Sarah. She reached for his hand, and he took it, gladly.

"Listen to me, James," Sarah said. "What happened here all those years ago was not your fault. It was a madness beyond your ability to help. It was a madness that had a life of its own. And your being turned, well, that was on Geoffrey, wasn't it? How could you blame yourself? You couldn't have guessed what Geoffrey had in mind that night." She brushed the stray gold hair from her husband's eyes and she kissed his forehead. "I absolve you, James John Wentworth. I absolve you of any guilt you may still feel. I accept you the way you are, and I understand why you're struggling being human again. We'll figure it out together, just like we've figured everything out together. Despite all the odds, we found our way back to each other. We have Grace back, and we have Johnny now. Don't you see? After everything, we are so lucky."

Olivia knelt beside them. "I just spoke to Martha, and the children are fine." She took James and Sarah's hands and joined them in her own. "Sarah is right, James. You are absolved. We don't need the universe to bring suffering to us. All too often we bring our suffering on ourselves. We are given the means to make sense of our lives. To learn lessons. To do better next time. Sometimes we understand the lessons and we do improve. Sometimes we pretend we don't see the signs until we're caught in a tsunami and our lives explode and we have no choice but to change. Sometimes we ignore the signs altogether and continue treating ourselves, and others, like expendable beings. No matter what, being grateful is always the best way. Be thankful to have your Lizzie back as Sarah. Be thankful for your children. Be thankful for your heartbeat and your flowing blood. Be grateful, James. Let go of the past, once and for all, for your sake, and for Sarah's. You simply cannot carry this guilt around any longer."

In that moment, as quick as the whispering wind, James felt the debilitating emotions from the past lift from his shoulders and float away across the bay. He had found that cloud Olivia told him about after all. He realized, with a smile, that he was ready to move forward toward everything good in his life. And he knew, staring into Sarah's eyes, that he had so much to look forward to. He would spend his life with his dear and loving wife. He would see his children grow. The possibilities were endless, he knew.

Sarah took his hand. "The shadows, James."

James shook his head. "What do you mean?"

"The shadows that have been haunting you. Where are they?"

The sun was dropping in the sky, so low that James thought if he reached out he could touch it. He turned to see the shadows behind him, where they belonged.

"It's like I said," Olivia said. "When you focus on one thing, you don't see the others. When you focus on the dark, you don't see the light. Light cannot exist without dark. You wouldn't recognize joy if you've never felt sorrow. How could you appreciate good if you did not know evil? In your dreams you equated shadows with monsters. But shadows are reflections cast by trees and houses. And people, James. Shadows are cast by people. If there were no people in your life, people like Sarah, then, yes, there would be no shadows. Do you want to live in a world without the beautiful, life-affirming trees? Without the people you love? Without Sarah?"

"Of course not," James said.

"Then you must accept the dark with the light. The evil with the good. You decide where to put your focus. If you focus on love, then that will be the purpose of your life. Focus on love, dear. Focus on Sarah and the children."

James smiled at his wife. He laughed when he realized how light he felt.

"I will," he said.

CHAPTER 19

James wasn't surprised to see his grandfather outside Olivia's house that night, but then nothing about Geoffrey surprised him. Geoffrey bowed in his courtly manner when James opened the door.

"It's wonderful to see you, Grandson. I do so enjoy seeing my human people."

"You just saw me last week, Geoffrey," James said.

"Yes, well, time flies. How are the littlest human people?"

"They're fine, Geoffrey," Sarah said.

"Wonderful! I'm glad to have my family back in Salem."

"I still wish you'd live with us in California," Sarah said.

"I would like that very much, but I can see my grandson isn't wholly enthralled with the idea, and I don't want to be in the way."

"Since when do you mind being in the way?" James asked.

"You won't be in the way," Sarah said. She looked sternly at James, who shrugged. "We have space in the backyard to build you a room. You should be with your family."

Geoffrey smirked at James. "Well, Tiddlywinks? What say you?"

"I thought you were Tiddlywinks," James said.

"No, young sir, I am Grandfather to you. Though I don't want to press you. Let me know what you decide."

Olivia came out of the kitchen, wiping her hands on a dish towel, smiling at the sight of her friend. "Geoffrey! How wonderful to see you. How are you, dear?"

"Very well, witchy woman, very well." Geoffrey squinted at James. "So? How did it go today? Did you spit on Hathorne's grave? Did you twinkle on his name? I certainly would have."

"How did you know I was at the cemeteries?" James asked. "I went during the day."

"Geoffrey knows everything," Olivia said. "Like I do."

"I didn't spit on anything," James said, "but thank you."

"Or twinkle?"

James tried to respond with his usual impatience but he couldn't stop laughing. "No, Geoffrey, I didn't twinkle, though I'd be lying if I didn't admit that the thought occurred to me."

"There you are. See? Take after your old grandsire, after all." Geoffrey stepped closer to James, squinting. "You do look different somehow. And what about those wicked shadows?"

Sarah took James' hand and he kissed her cheek. She smiled at him, a deep, true smile, one that radiated outward from that iridescent thread that bound them together all those years ago. They were still intertwined. They would always be. James did not doubt that now, and neither did Sarah, he knew. He kissed her again, and she laughed. Everywhere he looked that night he saw that radiant light, and he understood gratitude as he never had before.

"I feel free," James said.

"Facing your fears is always the best way through," Olivia said. "Yes, it's the most painful way, but unless you're clear with yourself about your emotions, and unless you allow yourself to feel them, then you'll never allow yourself to move forward, and that's what life is about—moving forward. Now that you've faced the anguish head-on, it's your turn, James. It's your turn to bask in the glow of this family that loves you, and it's time for you to embrace the everlasting love you have for them. You can leave the horrors of the witch hunts and all the miseries they brought you and Elizabeth behind. But you have to make the decision that you're going to face the sun, that you're going to focus on the positive, that you're going to open your heart to the vibrant colors around you. Life contains good and bad for everyone. It's up to us where we put our attention."

Sarah brushed some unruly gold locks from James' eyes. "Olivia is right, James. Being grateful doesn't mean we pretend that everything is always wonderful. It means that we acknowledge what is hard and painful but we still choose to focus on what is right and beautiful."

"So that's it?" Geoffrey asked. "All those years of poor me, yadda yadda yadda, and he goes to the graveyards and now he's all happy and shiny without a care in the world?"

"It's not that simple," Olivia said. "James took a necessary step today by facing down those memories that have been haunting him. The pain from that time will always be there, just as they are always there for Sarah. He's acknowledged the horrors by standing before them and telling them everything he had kept bottled up for so many years. Now whenever he's faced with the nightmares he can decide to focus on them or not. To be weighted down by them or not. He has the ability now to choose to focus on the present moment, and this present moment is pretty special if you ask me. James and Sarah have a happy life together." Olivia took James' hand. "This moment is all we truly have."

James smiled at the woman he loved most in the world. There she was, nodding at him, crying tears of joy, her kind-hearted, solid presence enough to warm his beating heart every day for the rest of his mortal existence. The pain from the past was just that. Past. He chose to focus on that moment. Holding Sarah's hand, he watched Olivia drink tea while Geoffrey peeked around the open door at the sleeping children. There were decisions to be made, of course. Would they take their home back from the Salem Historical Society and move back to Massachusetts? Would he keep his position at Berkeley and stay in California? What would they tell the children about their past? Would they tell Grace and Johnny that James had fallen in love with a beautiful farmer's daughter named Elizabeth Jones in 1691? And then they were reunited more than 300 years later? Would they tell their children about their love story that transcends time? And Grace had the right to know her story. She was the baby who died with Lizzie, after all.

The thought of telling Grace made James shudder. But that was another worry for another day. If James had learned anything from this experience, it was, as Olivia said, that this moment is all there is. He took his wife into his arms and exhaled, a long, slow moment of relief. The past was another life. Fate reunited James and Sarah after oh so very long. It had to be fate. What was the word Olivia used to describe their relationship? *Beshert*. They were soulmates, destined to be together.

James allowed himself the relief of basking in the glory that was his life with Sarah, the Grace they had been missing, and their baby boy. He knew not to take anything, his wife, his children, or his very mortal life, for granted. He knew all too well how all of it could be taken from him at any moment, sometimes for no reason at all.

Be here now, James thought. And he was.

I AM SITTING in the great room watching Lizzie bake Father his favorite vanilla cake. She measures the ingredients, whisks everything together, removes the hot pan carefully from the red-yellow cinders in the hearth, and pours in the batter. She shoos the cat away with a broom, afeared for the silly creature near the open flame. I have put my book down, finding such gladsomeness simply watching her. She hums to herself as she works and does not seem to notice me. She is the most dear thing to me. Simply being near her brings such contentedness, more than I ever thought possible in this preposterous world. Whilst there is madness outside my walls, inside is joy and laughter. And love.

I look at the goodness in my life and know I am the most fortunate of men. Even the frost-pinching cold of a Salem winter is alleviated by the heat emanating from the hearth and the warmth of devotion binding Lizzie and me together by an iridescent faerie-like thread. We are coiled together forever. Of this I have no doubt.

Lizzie notices me and smiles, amused by my rapt attention to her mundane task.

"Have you nothing better to do, Husband?" she asks.

"I have not," I say. "There is nowhere else in this world I'd rather be than beside you. There is nothing else I'd rather do than watch you. There is no one else I'd rather speak to than you."

She nods shyly as she pushes her skirts between her legs so they don't catch fire as she places the cake pan in the hearth.

"I feel the same about you," she whispers.

With her words I feel deep contentedness bubbling outward. I could dream about going back to Cambridge and completing my studies, which I have. I could think about everything in Massachusetts I dislike, a rather long list. I long to return to England, though I am well aware that troubles brew on that side of the Atlantic as well. But this moment is enough. Sitting near my hearth with my wife by my side, enjoying our time together, knowing that she feels for me as I feel for her.

This is all I need.

AUTHOR'S NOTES

Every time I think I'm finished writing *Loving Husband* books, fans ask for more. I try to be obliging when I can. In fact, the story behind *And Shadows Will Fall* was inspired by a fan.

When I finished writing the *Loving Husband Trilogy*, I thought I was done with the Wentworths' world. The story was complete in my mind and there was nothing left to say. Readers continued to ask very politely for more James and Sarah stories. For a long while, as in several years, my answer was, "That's all folks."

In time, I realized that I had more to say about the Wentworths' time in Salem during the witch hunts. As a result, the prequel, *Down Salem Way*, was born. Then an idea for a time travel story involving the Wentworths occurred to me, and the sequel, *The Duchess of Idaho*, was born.

Somewhere between the publication of *Down Salem Way* and *The Duchess of Idaho*, a kindly fan said, I bet James had a lot of problems after he became human again. It couldn't have been an easy adjustment after living a paranormal life for more than 300 years. Couldn't you write a book about that?

I thanked the fan profusely, and I was indeed grateful. The fact that fans love the *Loving Husband Trilogy* enough that they think of new ways to continue the story is every writer's dream. At the time, I was working on *Christmas at Hembry Castle*, then *Painting the Past*, and then *The Duchess of Idaho*. After I finished *The Duchess of Idaho*, my thoughts went back to that fan's suggestion.

Why couldn't I write that story? I realized that maybe something was missing, some link between *Her Loving Husband's Return* and *The*

Duchess of Idaho. Once I made that connection, *And Shadows Will Fall* had to be written. There was no way around it.

And Shadows Will Fall proved to be a particularly interesting book to write since it has several moving parts. Olivia takes center stage, as she does whenever she's invited into a story, good old Olivia. Another reader suggested a prequel about Olivia. I'd be lying if I didn't admit that I think it's a great idea. *And Shadows Will Fall* continues James and Sarah's story after the conclusion of *Her Loving Husband's Return*, Book 3 of the *Loving Husband Trilogy*, while it also has elements of James' diary from the late seventeenth century as we see in *Down Salem Way*. A few clues about the time-travel sequel, *The Duchess of Idah*o, also make an appearance. In many ways, *And Shadows Will Fall* is the piece that ties the *Loving Husband* stories together.

And Shadows Will Fall wasn't meant to be a stand-alone, unlike *Down Salem Way* or *The Duchess of Idaho*, both of which were written so readers wouldn't have to be familiar with the trilogy. *And Shadows Will Fall* was intended for readers of the trilogy, which is why I wrote this novella as a love letter to the *Loving Husband Trilogy* fans.

Thank you to the fan who suggested the idea for *And Shadows Will Fall*. And thank you to the James and Sarah fans all over the world who have been following the Wentworths for more than a decade. You are more appreciated than you will ever know.

ABOUT THE AUTHOR

Meredith Allard is an award-winning author known for the bestselling *Loving Husband Trilogy* and the Victorian novel *When It Rained at Hembry Castle,* which IndieReader named a Best Historical Novel. Her prequel, *Down Salem Way,* earned the B.R.A.G. Medallion and was a semi-finalist for the Chaucer Award in Early Historical Fiction.

A recognized authority on the craft, Meredith is the author of *Painting the Past: A Guide for Writing Historical Fiction,* a #1 Amazon New Release in Authorship and Creativity Self-Help. For over twenty years, she has mentored writers of all ages, helping them find their voices while honing her own signature blend of meticulous research and haunting prose.

When she isn't unearthing the secrets of the past, she can be found in the hills of Southern Nevada with her cats and a cup of coffee.

Join Meredith online at www.meredithallard.com for her weekly blog posts and monthly newsletter.

BOOKS BY MEREDITH ALLARD

And Shadows Will Fall

Christmas at Hembry Castle

Down Salem Way

The Duchess of Idaho

Her Dear & Loving Husband

Her Loving Husband's Curse

Her Loving Husband's Return

Painting the Past: A Guide for Writing Historical Fiction

The Professor of Eventide

The Swirl and Swing of Words: Embracing the Writing Life

Victory Garden

When It Rained at Hembry Castle

Woman of Stones

www.ingramcontent.com/pod-product-compliance
Lightning Source LLC
LaVergne TN
LVHW090612110826
845146LV00001B/362

* 9 7 9 8 2 1 8 4 1 6 0 2 7 *